"Modesta is a gifted story teller. A beautiful writer. A woman with a vision who can articulate life into words on a page that will take you on a journey. A journey of love, betrayal and sisterhood. It is passionate, alluring, exciting, intimate and emotionally raw. It is not only a story it is an experience. A must read."

—Tania Joy Antonio
Canadian Author

"*I Love You Still* by Modesta Tonan is the perfect sequel to *I Belong To You*. It leaves you in suspense and at the edge of your seat with every turn of the page. As a reader, picking sides between Anthony and Sebastian is seemingly difficult. It is refreshing to have a lead woman play a powerful yet vulnerable role packaged in Julia. The gradual escalation of her travels and being stuck between the past and the future is very relatable and the uncertainty leaves suspense and doubt throughout every turn of the page. The story is climatic and keeps you guessing right to the very end, while revealing the true meaning of love, life, and the challenges both men and women face in relationships. Julia's diaries and her openness to share every detail was a great addition. I Love You Still is a must read for all romance lovers everywhere."

—Mark Antidormi
Avid Reader

"What a book, full of excitement, and real life as I know it. Julia's journey reveals the struggles we all face in our relationships and daily life. True, honest, and passionate with each written word. Julia's journey is one filled with raw emotions and the rediscovery of her identity. Modesta's style of writing shows a deep passion for the arts. She brings us along to make us feel all of it with her, and we can all relate one way or another - Some of us may even question our own choices; and wonder if we are only meant to have one true love in our lifetime? A Must Read!"

—Catrin Moehwald
Critical Thinker in Entrepreneurial World

I Love You Still

Modesta Tonan

 FriesenPress

Suite 300 - 990 Fort St
Victoria, BC, V8V 3K2
Canada

www.friesenpress.com

Copyright © 2020 by Modesta Tonan
First Edition — 2020

All rights reserved.

Illustration by Lisa Vecchio Mollica

Photography by Nadia Trapasso Green - Dreams and Tales Fine Art

This book is a work of fiction. References to real people, events, establishments, and organizations are intended only to provide a sense of authenticity and are used fictitiously. All other characters, incidents, and dialogue are drawn from the author's imagination and should not be construed as real.

All rights reserved, including the right to reproduce this book or portions thereof in any form whatsoever. This book or parts thereof may not be reproduced in any form without permission from the author. Exceptions are made for brief excerpts used in published reviews.

www.modestatonan.com

ISBN
978-1-5255-7732-1 (Hardcover)
978-1-5255-7733-8 (Paperback)
978-1-5255-7734-5 (eBook)

1. FICTION, ROMANCE, LATER IN LIFE

Distributed to the trade by The Ingram Book Company

DEDICATION

(In Memoriam)

Of my mother, Teresa Vecchio

Your unconditional love has turned me into a story teller.

&

To My Person, Josephine Devellis

Thank you for your unwavering support and love

I could not have done this without you.

ACKNOWLEDGMENTS

I would like to thank the following people:

My husband Marino. Your love and encouragement get me through the hardest moments of my life. You have shown me how powerful love can be. Your support has allowed me to be a true artist and to create and explore my passion for storytelling. I'm forever grateful for you and our beautiful children, Lucas, Isabella, and Ava. I look forward to growing old with you and having many more adventures. "I Love You Still."

To "SOFT" Lisa, Nora, Alana, Josie, and Astrid. Thank you for being my muses. You are all strong and remarkable women. You are my friends, family, and the other half of my life. I Love Us.

I would like to express a special thanks of gratitude to my friend Adele, not only for her guidance, generosity, and belief in me, but for teaching me to stand by my choices and to always remember "my why." I look forward to the next part of our journey together.

To Mark, thank you for giving me a male's point of view. You always came to my rescue when I just didn't know "how." Your expertise always got me out of a bind. You have taught me to be a better writer, and I thank you for that.

Finally, I'm extremely grateful to my parents for their love, prayers, and sacrifices. They have taught me that family comes first and that love matters. They have instilled in me the culture and traditions of beautiful Italia. I always hope to have passionate love in my life like you both have had in yours, the kind that continues beyond death. I Love You Forever.

CONTENTS

A New Life 1
Montauk 4
Canada 19
Montauk 36
White Sheets, Canada 40
Forget-Me-Not 49
See Me 61
Home 67
Christmas 74
The Bello Wedding 81
The Whole Truth 90
Soft Sisters in Ireland 103
Positano 115
Ravello 124
The Villa 134
Grocery Store 142
Revelations 154
Secrets 166
The Choice 175
The Duel 181

I Love You Still

A NEW LIFE

Do not go … But if you must … Take my soul with you.

Rumi

September

I can't seem to escape neither my sins, nor my choices. Love had led me to rediscovering myself, and now that very stirring experience of my own free will has left me with nothing but a heap of lies, haunting memories, and the yearning to surrender to them—surrender to him.

What ruin I have created in my perfect white-picket-fenced world. How can I ever be the same, and why would I want to be? After all, Sebastian saved me from myself, from an undeniably sad and lonely life. And yet, at times, I feel tortured. The very essence of my eternal being continually searches for a way to rationalize and validate my relationship with the man.

Once upon a time I loved my life; I loved life in general. But now conflicting emotions consume everything that was once beautiful about me. Every morning I question the woman staring back at me in the mirror: *Who are you? My god Julia, what have you done?*

At times, I feel withdrawn and invisible to the world.

A crumbling marriage to Anthony, a much-needed adventure to Verona in Italy with my soul sisters … that was six months ago. I was hoping to rediscover who I was while trying to recapture a small piece of that woman. The secrets of that journey, however, are now both the delicious memories and the deeply embedded scars that have come to define who I am today.

I now must embark upon another personal quest to rediscover this new and forever changed version of me. No one has the right to judge me or my actions. I own my journey, and only I can empower and control my feelings and the outcome, be what it may, with Anthony and Sebastian.

I try to stop these overwhelming feelings and thoughts. I tell myself: *You need to regain control of your heart and somehow trust that same heart that led you astray.* But how can you really trust that which feeds on tumultuous passions and inspired magical whims? I have been both blessed and cursed by two immensely handsome, passionate men who adore the ground I walk upon. How can I not want and need them both?

The scent of betrayal hovers over me. It haunts me every single day and night. That echoing voice that keeps reminding me: *Julia what have you done?*

The core of me wants to surrender into the arms of Sebastian, yet something holds me back. Is it the thought of losing my first love, my children, family, and friends? Or, is there something more at stake? If the underlying truth surfaces, my world will be forever changed.

Why must it be so difficult to navigate the waters of love, emotion, and honesty? Why can't we just engage in seemingly endless conversations with those we care about and openly share each moment as it occurs? Oh, if only this was a reality! It would be the perfect solution for my aching heart.

I'm a married woman with a beautiful family and a blessed past. Yet I ache to be ignited by Sebastian's passionate ways and intriguing conversations. I want to be with him. I want to get lost in his piercing green eyes and be wrapped in the tender warmth of his body.

My love for him is now inextricable from my soul and it refuses to allow me to shut the door on "a new life," as my mind helpfully refers to it; even if that means living with eternal judgment should my secret life of lies be revealed.

The voices won't stop talking in my head. *My god Julia, you're in love with two men!*

Julia

MONTAUK

"Maybe … you will fall in love with me all over again." "Hell," I said, "I love you enough now. What do you want to do? Ruin me?" "Yes. I want to ruin you." "Good," I said. "That's what I want too."

Ernest Hemingway

Anthony's plan to take me away for the weekend to Montauk, one of our favorite hideaways in the Hamptons, reignited my inner passion. It had been far too long since we had gone away together, and I had found myself looking forward to the trip with an unexpected girlish glee. The anticipation reminded me of when our relationship was new and suffused with giddy spontaneity. Before the "normalcy" of the everyday set in, before the recognition that we had all the time in the world to love and appreciate each other in every way. Surprises that would bring either one of us a smile of such brightness and beauty that the people around us couldn't help but smile too.

I LOVE YOU STILL

On occasion, there were still remnants of this type of joy. Anthony showed it in small ways: the brush of his hand against mine, the tucking of my hair behind my ear, a small kiss on top of my head, the silent promise of love and continued affection. I responded in kind, trying to push down the voices bubbling up inside telling me that, somehow, I was wrong. We had been through so much together after all.

I had been so happy when he informed me of the trip. We were lying in bed, our fingers entwined, resting on the pillow between us. He whispered to me of his surprise. Every now and then, one of us would shift forward a little, gently kissing the knuckles of the other.

"I want us to go back there," he had said. "Do you remember when we were young, without a care in the world?" So, I had packed enthusiastically, Anthony playfully kissing my forehead. He knew how much this trip meant to me.

Montauk was a hidden gem, a beautiful place with a cool, laidback vibe and more than a hint of sophistication. The small town's simplicity allowed us as a couple to truly relax and connect with one another. The food and drink were out of this world, especially the locally caught fresh fish and local wine.

In an album at home, I had pictures from every trip that we had taken to my favorite winery, one we had first visited on our honeymoon. These reminded me of what had first started as romantic visits, watching golden sunsets, and ending in us making passionate love. Over time, they showed the smiling couple growing older but still sparkling as we held up our glasses of wine.

That he had remembered my love of Montauk and arranged a special weekend meant everything to me. The beach house was perfect, with a stunning ocean view, but before long the voices in my head were there, compelling me to question whether I should even be in that place, in that room. The sudden feeling of guilt sent shivers down my spine. I was completely overwhelmed. I stood half-dressed, staring out the window overlooking the ocean waves. I wondered why life couldn't be as free-spirited as that water, calmly drifting in and out.

It seemed like hours, yet only minutes had passed, as I became one with the ocean, embracing its beauty and the fierce nature it represented. I had never really given it much thought, how similar my situation mirrored that of the ocean's disposition. I listened and gazed at this beautiful creation of God, completely lost in the hypnotizing sound and magic; it calmed my mind. I felt very much like Salacia, goddess of the sea, personified by the calm of the water and the wonder of the sun lighting it. The swirling greens and blues felt part of me. *Was Anthony supposed to be my Neptune?* I wondered.

The waves were continuously crashing on the rocks and the sandy beach line of the resort, as reality quickly sunk in, my thoughts immediately racing back to the uncertainty I felt in my heart. Could we save our marriage? Could the concept of "us" be saved after twenty-five years of friendship, love, and raising our family?

Julia, you have to keep it together, the little voice kept instructing me. I knew this could be our last chance to reconnect, to finally take the time needed to rekindle the passion that had been lost over the years, given the typical upsets and detours of marriage. I wanted to be at peace with my decision to embrace this time with Anthony and remove the barriers; I wanted us to become transparent and vulnerable during this weekend together.

I LOVE YOU STILL

In the distance I could hear the horns from the ocean liners as they passed the beach house on their way to some spectacular destination, no doubt. I couldn't help it, try as I might, my imagination won out, and it kept pulling me back to my last night with Sebastian …

He kissed the back of my neck and I shivered as he slipped my dress off my shoulder. With tiny, nibbling kisses he explored the newly bare flesh. I couldn't move, nor did I want to. With a confident trace of his finger, my other strap fell. I couldn't help but moan as his eyes lustfully took in the tops of my breasts. He could smell my arousal while drinking in my near-frenzied state, and I turned to push myself up against him. I felt the rough touch of fabric rubbing against my flesh, his hardness pressing against my stomach.

Our lips met forcefully, his tongue thrusting against mine as he pulled me in tighter. Heat shot through me; I knew there was no turning back. Our desire for each other had become so strong, so magnetic. I left his luscious lips to focus on his neck, relishing the deep moan that left his throat. I could feel the vibrations against my lips.

At that moment, I became everything that he wanted me to be. He pushed me against the wall, the sensation of being trapped by such erotic fervor making me feel more sensual and beautiful than I ever had before. He held my hands above my head, and I totally surrendered. I wanted nothing more than to taste, touch, and feel everything with him.

"Sei bellissima amore. Ti amo. Stasera, domani, per sempre," he whispered.

He picked me up, walked over to his bed and laid me down. I watched as he undressed, his eyes never leaving mine. I anticipated my lover, and he knew the power he had over me.

He wanted me, and I needed him. Our bodies intertwined, and his intense thrusts were matched by my own.

It thrilled me, he thrilled me; I wanted more.

Without realizing it, I let out a sigh that was reflective of the desperate longing inside me. I shook myself from these thoughts. I was going to make us late for dinner. Yes, leave it to me to never be on time; it was one of those qualities that drove my husband crazy.

How would I ever manage to maintain my composure at dinner this evening? I truly feared our life together was too far gone and had been so for many years now. How had this happened to us? Were we not the same people who had sat together in that vineyard, enamored by the simplicity of the sunset and delicious wine? We had changed, but was that a bad thing?

Part of me would always crave Anthony's musky smell. I missed him, and I needed to feel him again, and not just the touch of his hands on my body, but his brilliant comfort and familiarity. He made me feel safe in a way that no other man could. Did that make up for the excitement and anticipation that came with the newness and unknown of an emerging relationship?

I closed my eyes and imagined how Anthony and I would end our evening—making love, coming together under the night sky, the sound of the waves rolling in, matching our rhythm. I felt fiercely sensual by the freedom my new

I LOVE YOU STILL

confidence gave me. I was no longer the shy, unsure girl that had fallen for the seemingly mature and experienced Anthony. Before, I had allowed him to take the lead, to take me to new and dizzying heights. Now I was able to do the same for him.

I enjoyed tormenting him with my previously unfamiliar, seductive ways. And yet there was still that gap, something missing. As much as I tried to think only of Anthony while we were making love, a part of me always drifted back to Sebastian. Admittedly, these thoughts of my lover made me freer with my husband. Anthony loved this newfound wife of his. Pleasure was indeed my punishment.

It was wrong, surely, to envision another man sighing so sweetly on top of me, shaking the bed with the force of his thrusts. It was wrong to see the intensity in his eyes as he kept them open to look at me, moaning words of lustful delirium. There was no reason that my thoughts should stray, and yet there was every reason in the world. Tonight though, I would focus on Anthony, and Anthony alone. I would concentrate on remaining present. Afterward, I would smooth his hair flat and curl up against him, feeling the soreness of my muscles from the exertion of our passion. It would be just like old times.

I slipped into my little black Chanel dress and put on my favorite pair of silver Jimmy Choo pumps. My ears were adorned with pearl earrings, a gift from Anthony on our twelfth wedding anniversary. I applied mascara, drew a careful line over my lips with a simple gloss, and allowed my dark hair to hang in loose waves around my face.

Simplicity and elegance were part of what Anthony loved about me. Often, he would say that I lit up the room when I walked into it, emphatically assuring me that I was the most beautiful woman there. The wonderful thing was that I believed that to him I probably was. He also loved to hear the echo of my voice and laughter. I still remembered him once saying, "Julia, you can be heard for miles and could warm the coldest hearts." I knew he was as proud of me as I was of him. I only wished that pride had kept me from falling in love with another man.

The guest room door slowly opened; Anthony stood there silently, just staring as if it were the first time that he had laid eyes on me. I felt the intensity of his gaze as it graced every curve of my body. Before I could grasp the moment fully, Anthony's strong arms embraced me, and he whispered into my ear, "You look so beautiful, Julia."

My face was slightly flushed as little butterflies danced a graceful waltz in my stomach. The Anthony here, now, left me with a feeling of uncertainty and intense excitement for our time in Montauk. Our eyes met slowly as we began to pull away from each other. The memories of so many years ago came rushing back with such fierceness that I honestly wasn't capable of rational thought. That feeling alone was priceless. Here we were again, seeing each other as if we were meeting for the very first time. At this very moment, nothing, not even Sebastian seemed important anymore.

Sometimes, it was as if I could genuinely see into the depths of Anthony's soul. And in those moments, I felt most connected to him. Such moments made me wonder when and why I had lost him. Did I not show him enough affection? Had he strayed from me too? Was he also thinking of another when he was with me? So many questions; they never stopped coming into my thoughts.

Anthony looked better now than he ever had. The weight loss served him quite well, slight hints of muscle rippled through the Hugo Boss shirt that otherwise hung loosely over his black dress pants. His distinguished salt and pepper hair had grown out longer since I had left for Italy, and now it gracefully shaped his face, bringing out his chiseled Italian features.

As I ran my fingers through his silvery locks, he asked me, somewhat self-consciously, "Julia, should I color my hair?"

"No! I'll kill you if you do! Jesus, Anthony, you look so good. Haven't you heard of the allure of the silver fox?" I teased playfully. "Forget coloring it—I like you exactly as you are right now."

He was sexy, really sexy. Part of him knew this, and yet part of him, I think, felt insecure when it came to growing older. I had never understood my husband's sensitivities regarding his age. He smiled broadly. A compliment, a small amount of reassurance, and his fears were alleviated, for now. I wondered whether maybe I didn't offer this enough.

"I love you too, Julia," he replied softly, lowering his lips to mine in a gentle, lingering kiss.

Slowly, he released his grip; our dinner reservations were for 7 p.m. at one of our favorite restaurants in town. South Madison never failed to deliver the perfect evening: a joyful, relaxed atmosphere and excellent food.

"We should get going Julia. I don't like to be late, and I'm hungry."

I knew that my Anthony was trying, and I was willing to try to give my heart to him as completely as I had when our relationship began. I used to spend hours cooking for him, trying to recreate the dishes that he had gushed about on our trips. The thought of lobster and scallops made me realize that I was quite hungry as well.

I smiled and turned to the mirror once more, a final check of my appearance. If I ever wanted to truly be the most beautiful woman in the room to my husband, it was tonight.

"I'll meet you in the lobby. I need to have a quick talk with the concierge about our reservation," he said before leaving.

The door clicked shut behind him, and the air in the room shifted. An overwhelming sense of stillness set in. Alone with such silence it was inevitable that my thoughts again drifted to Sebastian. I knew that I should check my text messages. Sebastian had responded to an earlier text that I had sent him. I had turned my phone off during the trip to Montauk in fear of him sending me messages while I was with Anthony. A secret life comes with a lot of rules and learned deception. It was at times so hard to keep up with that it exhausted me. How would I ever tell him that it was now over? I knew I had to stop this emotional roller coaster. I owed it to my marriage, to Anthony, and to myself.

As I looked in the mirror, I realized that I no longer truly knew the woman staring back. And at that very moment, my cell phone began to vibrate. *I'm not looking. I refuse to look.* I wanted to turn it off again, but I just couldn't. I unzipped my clutch and dropped the phone inside. My hands were shaking as I attempted a last touch up. It was then, glancing at my smudged lips, that I knew I had to read Sebastian's messages.

```
My dearest Julia. I miss the taste of your
sweet lips and the scent of your perfume.
I miss grabbing your beautiful dark hair
with my hands as I make love to you. Ah,
my beautiful lady, the bed linens are still
soaked from the heat of our passion. The
```

```
taste of your sweet nectar still remains on
my lips. I can't stop thinking about you.
Ti amo.
```

He had sent it the night before. Before my text about Montauk. I had to close my eyes to regain my composure. I would never understand the seemingly infinite grip he had on my mind and body. I had convinced myself that the right thing to do was to stay with Anthony. Yet I knew that my soul unconditionally and overwhelmingly would always belong to Sebastian.

Suddenly my phone again began to ring; I answered it. It was Anthony.

"Hurry up, Jules. Dinner in five minutes."

"Sorry, I'm coming."

Julia, breathe, take a deep breath, relax, I told myself. I quickly attempted to gather my belongings and raced down the hall toward the elevator. Why did I always have to be late? Just once, I wished I could stay focused. Reading Sebastian's message had distracted me, and now I was left hurrying to have dinner with my husband. I would find time to text him back later tonight.

As the elevator door began to open, I glanced one last time at my phone—a recent text message came in from Sebastian:

```
Julia, you're all I need to breathe, and
yet I find myself gasping for air. I'm alone
here even when I'm with you and it hurts
that I can't have all of you because you're
with him. For that reason, I've decided
to return to Italy. You have made it very
clear to me where your priority will always
lie. I promise you this, my love, for as
```

```
long as you're with him, no matter how many
times you touch him, it's me you will think
about. I'll never be able to say goodbye to
you my love. Until we meet again.

My eternal love
```

The elevator door opened. Quickly, I pushed the button to close it before Anthony could see me. An intense sadness flooded over me; I couldn't breathe. I was hyperventilating, pressing my hands and forehead against the cool mirror. I was tormented by thoughts of my decision to tell Sebastian about the surprise weekend away with Anthony, by text no less. What was I thinking? He deserved more from me. I had left him feeling alone. I never meant to hurt him. In some strange way I knew he would want me to be happy at any cost, regardless of his own pain. Despite, or perhaps because of his love for me, Sebastian seemed to cling to this internal remorse for interfering in my family life. He knew it would forever create a divide that would destroy me, should our secret ever come to light.

He had never mentioned my physically connecting to my husband before, not like this at any rate. That fire, that intensity. He deliberately meant to hurt me with those words. I had opened the door for him—Sebastian—in a way brought me back to life. He had made me fall in love with him, and now he was leaving me. I suddenly felt so lost and helpless, and unable to stop him.

The elevator door opened, and Anthony walked toward me. He took my hand and hurried us toward the lobby. "What took you so long? I was beginning to worry. Are you okay? You look pale," he said.

"I'm okay. I er, I'm sorry, I just er forgot my phone and ran back to the room to get it in case the kids need to get a hold of us." *Get it together Julia.* The voice in my head was right. I couldn't believe how easy the words rolled off my tongue. The guilt bubbled once again, but I somehow pushed it down and apologetically touched his arm.

"Julia let's just enjoy the evening together. The kids are fine." As he gently kissed my lips, he whispered, "You're all mine tonight."

We entered the restaurant; I tried to maintain my composure despite still reeling with the thought of Sebastian's decision to leave. I was planning to end our secret life anyway, right?

South Madison glowed with low-hanging lights, providing a dimmed, intimate setting; we were seated at a window overlooking the ocean—the waves before us, a hint of sea breeze hitting us through the opened windows. Despite it still being early, the restaurant was busy, but our small world was secluded. I reached for Anthony's hand while we read through the menu. The details were perfect, from the low sunlight to the bottle of wine already waiting. Anthony had the concierge order it in advance; a small gesture, one I appreciated. Christian's Cuvée was my favorite Merlot; the taste of this classic wine had subtle hints of oak and cherry on the nose and dark chocolate that melded beautifully with the smells of sea salt, and fresh fish.

Wine had always been the thread that kept Anthony and me sane, oiling us in ways that allowed us to cast off any veneers and talk with ease.

"Julia, Julia?" Anthony's voice from across the table echoed as he tried to get my attention.

"Oh! I'm sorry." I hadn't noticed the waitress was ready to pour my wine. I pulled myself back into the present, focusing on my husband. He had begun to flirt with our pretty sommelier. I had to get his attention back.

"Anthony," I said, as my hand slightly began to tremble holding my empty glass. "Maybe we should let her pour the wine."

Without hesitation, Anthony responded, "Yes, of course."

I knew that whatever changes I had gone through, Anthony also had to deal with his own demons. I imagined he too was struggling to find out who he was again. I had to give him the benefit of the doubt. Looking wasn't the same as touching. And my husband *had* always been engaging and charming. People gravitated toward him.

I carefully raised the glass to smell the unique flavors that had taken years to acquire. I always tried to lose myself in the heart of the wine. It really is a craft after all, and I had the utmost respect for the science of wine. Thoughts disappeared with my first sip.

"Delicious! God, I love this wine!"

Anthony put his own glass down whilst straightening the napkin on his lap. He coughed quietly.

"Jules, what do you think about you and me drinking wine in Italy next year? It's been so long since we took a real vacation without the kids."

"Excuse me? What?" Stumbling over my words, I nearly choked on my wine. I didn't know how much more I could take. First Sebastian announcing he was leaving me and now my husband wants us to have a romantic holiday in Italy no less. What the fuck is going on?

"I just know how much you love Italy, and I thought maybe it's time we experienced it together. I told you I want to do more things with you. Don't you want that too? Julia are you sure you're okay? You seem distant."

"I'm fine Anthony, just shocked." How could I possibly disappoint him? After all, he was right, that was what I yearned for. I wanted to spend more time with him. A chance to rekindle our love, to discover new things, places, and each other. Our last few years together had become difficult, filled more with regret and resentment than anything else. It sometimes felt so right, but also so wrong. And yet, how could Italy become a place for Anthony and me, when it held so many memories of Sebastian?

"Julia, look at me. What are you worried about?"

I thought quickly. "I'm just concerned about the girls' trip scheduled for next summer. You know I can't back out of it now. It's too late."

"Is that what you're worried about? You can still do your birthday trip with the girls; I thought I could come and meet you once they return. Jules, I can't do it before. Work is crazy busy this summer, and I've already scheduled time off. I knew you wouldn't say no. You can organize all the details. You're good at that. I want you to book us into that little town you fell in love with and have been talking about for the last year—Ravello right? I want to see why you love it so much and, of course, let's visit some wineries. I just want to experience all of the magic with you."

Before I could answer him, the waitress came over to take our order and refill our glasses. She couldn't have come at a better time, allowing me to gather my senses. After she left us alone, I answered Anthony with one word, clutching tightly to the hand that still held mine.

"Yes!"

He replied softly, "I love you Jules, more than you will ever know. All I want is for us to be happy and do the things that we always talked about."

We continued our conversation about Italy and we also talked about our son's upcoming wedding. We soon began to eat, and that's when I remembered that I hadn't deleted Sebastian's last messages. I would probably be reading them over and over again, trying to convince myself that it would be alright. I would delete them later and do my best to try to forget about him. After all, that's what he wanted me to do.

CANADA

Forgiveness is the remission of sins. For it is by this that what has been lost, and found, is saved from being lost again.

St. Augustine

Six months earlier

Marriage is not without issues and compromise. My life has become overly complicated to the point where not even I can truly comprehend the full magnitude of this continuous loop of lies I have slowly created. As time moves forward, the pattern becomes less of habit and more of need. I tend to talk to myself more than normal lately; I wonder whether the voices in my mind are all that keep me from going insane. *Just leave Anthony and run away with Sebastian, never look back,* the voice prompts. What would life be like with him in Italy? And yet I stop myself from going there, scolding myself: *What the fuck are you thinking Julia? Anthony is your husband, the father of your children, and you do love him—why are you taking such unnecessary risks when you have everything you need?*

Julia

★ ★ ★

Sebastian ultimately decided to move to Canada to be closer to me. He took a sabbatical from his business and left his hometown, all for a relationship to this point sustained by text messages. I knew we felt the same though. Every time my phone vibrated and lit up with a new message, excitement coursed through me, my guilt only kept at bay by the rationalization that this was merely a continued correspondence between acquaintances, friends who had met in another part of the world. Because we were miles apart, I could justify it and consequently felt safe in my love for this man. I was also very curious about exactly who Sebastian DeLuca was.

I was worried about Anthony finding out of course. What if he happened upon my text messages? What if I accidentally sent him one meant for Sebastian? Nevertheless, I always made sure my phone was kept locked. We were having dinner, sitting across from each other at our kitchen table, when my phone lit up with a message that I knew was from Sebastian. I quickly snuck away to the kitchen to read it.

```
My love, I always miss you. I only have one
question for you. Please answer it hon-
estly. What do you want?
```

My heart exploded, and I quickly locked my phone. Anthony was staring at me, slowly chewing. It seemed wrong, the candles on the table and open bottle of wine. I couldn't quite hide my panic. I sat back down and reached for my glass, taking a long sip.

"Who was is it?" he asked, as I turned my attention back to my food. I smiled whilst twirling a forkful of spaghetti.

"It's just Francesca. She's going through some troubles at the moment." He nodded, seemingly satisfied with the lie; I let out a sigh of relief and added, "I'll probably invite her over for dinner tomorrow night. We can always go for a walk if we need to speak in private. You know, girl talk. She trusts you, of course, but this is quite delicate, it … ahh …"

"Will remain between friends. I don't want to know, and I don't need to know Jules," he accepted gently. "But don't worry. I'll be working late tomorrow. So, you will have the house to yourself."

"Again?"

"Sorry, Jules, but how do you our think our trips and your shoes get paid for?"

"Anthony!"

"I'm kidding. Don't get upset Jules." He walked over, kissed my forehead, told me he loved me, and walked away.

He had been working late more and more often. Before my trip to Italy, he could sometimes work late for an entire week and be unfazed that we had spent so little time together. I couldn't criticize him for it—he worked hard, in an excellent job. He supported us, provided a wonderful quality of life. I really had no reason to complain, and yet it hurt me just the same.

I had stopped questioning him about it, however. Since the children had left, it was probably natural that he put in more hours. Besides, given the situation, asking him to come home seemed utterly selfish on my part.

We had come to a delicate balance since my return; we were spending more time together and actively working to fix the marriage. And of course, I felt tremendous guilt for my affair. He felt guilt for the argument we had before I left. Possibly, who knows, for more than that, but I couldn't tell for sure.

To date that had been the worst night of my life and the worst fight of our marriage. Not because of the ugly words hurled back and forth necessarily, but because of the way it happened. Our children watching. Anthony, getting into a car drunk. Me looking desperately for him in the middle of the night, going from his office to the local hospitals. Remembering it was like a trance, as though remembering the most horrific and vaguest of nightmares.

Every hospital that hadn't admitted him gave me relief. And yet, every minute that I didn't find him, every place that he wasn't, gave me more pain. I couldn't possibly have known where he had gone. That, incidentally, was the first time that he had ever been physical—he had put his hands on me and pushed me to the floor. Alcohol played a big part in that terrible night. He hadn't done it since, but that memory was still the most vivid.

His anger during that fight opened my eyes to just how broken our life had become. A man who once only had eyes for me, was now openly flirting with other women. That wildly passionate and loving man had been reduced to a drunk driver. Apparently, he had needed perspective just as much as I did.

Since then, our daughter Mia had taken to phoning home far more often. While her sister Camilla kept to her usual schedule (every other Thursday), Mia always needed more reassurance, and the memory of her sobbing into her duvet while Camilla comforted her had been unbearable.

That fight had been my fault, our fault. We hadn't managed to keep that argument from the children. No matter how hard I had tried, it hadn't mattered. I had started the argument, and Anthony would always get the final word.

That night told me what I already knew, we both needed a break. He had gone to god knows where, with god knows who, while I waited at home, not sure whether he was alive or dead, or even whether I wanted him to return that night, but certain that I wanted him to be safe. Even when reflecting upon the pain, his hateful behavior, and his anger, I still loved him. I still wanted him to be okay.

And yet, I needed to be okay too. Didn't I deserve to feel happy and alive, to feel like me again? Staying in that house with his ever-increasing mood swings, the fights occurring more and more often, I couldn't. I wouldn't allow myself to be beaten down and have my self-esteem undermined by his flirtatious behavior and drinking habits. I had to look after my girls, and I had to look after myself.

But tonight, Anthony went to fetch another bottle of wine, and I quickly replied to Sebastian's message. Fueled by longing, missing the time that we had spent together in Italy, and sad that my husband still wasn't filling the void I felt, I replied as earnestly as I could.

```
You. I want you.
```

If I had known what would happen, what that message would lead to, would I still have sent it?

★ ★ ★

Francesca, my best friend, had always been one of the most compassionate people I had ever known, abounding in motherly concern for everyone and anyone, regardless of age and life experience. I could have wept when she waltzed into my home with a large metal container of gelato under one arm and prosecco under the other.

"Wow, you're a lifesaver," I sighed happily, grabbing a couple of spoons from the kitchen drawer and seating myself comfortably beside her on the sofa. I couldn't remember the last time that we had done this; cuddled up with glasses full to the brim and an open container of dessert between us.

Somehow Francesca always knew exactly what would cheer me up, and exactly where to find it. Gelato is something that's only really made well in Italy—I had tried numerous places during my travels, and the majority I had tasted came closer to ice cream than gelato. Even the ones that claimed to be "Italian style" had this artificialness to them. The metal container alone made me smile.

"Mmmmm," I moaned, completely satisfied, letting a spoonful hit my tongue. Pistachio, a favorite for both of us. It was the perfect brown-green color, with chopped nuts on top. "Where did you get this?"

She grinned and took a sip of her prosecco before replying, "You want me to take away the magic, m'lady? How can you enjoy it if you can have it every day?"

I laughed, letting the bubbles and the coolness of the gelato relax me. "You may keep your secret for as long as you keep bringing me the goods," I said.

"Only if you cough up. What's been happening? You sounded pretty desperate when you called me to come see you tonight. Is it to do with, you know …?" she trailed off.

I swallowed a mouthful of the delicious prosecco and returned my spoon to the tub, sobering.

"Yeah, it is. It's, well, we've still been messaging each other."

"And? I need details." Her tone was playful, but her face was full of such caring concern that tears sprang to my eyes.

"I just … I just don't know what to do," I whispered. "It was supposed to be over, and now it seems like neither of us wants it to be."

Fran handed me my glass, and a tissue from the box on the coffee table. I dabbed at my eyes and took a deep breath before continuing.

"I just don't know what I want anymore. Things with Anthony have been better since I got back, you know. I've been trying really hard, and I think he has too. I don't want to ruin that."

"But you also don't want to let go of Sebastian," Fran said, nodding. "How do you feel about him? You should be more certain of your feelings now that you're apart. Jules, listen honey, Alessandro sent me this quote the other day that I want to share with you. 'Absence sharpens love, presence strengthens it.' Beautiful and accurate."

"That's so true! I miss him Fran. I want to see him again. I need to know what we are. I know it's fucked up. I thought the distance would have eventually lessened my thoughts of him and our time together. But instead, the time apart has only made it harder. I do love Anthony. No one knows me better than my husband, and we've gone through so much together. It's familiar comfort … you know what I mean? I do want us to be happy again; it just feels like so much has transpired over the years. We've created a life together, a family, and now it seems as if my heart is split in two.

"How can I feel so much for Sebastian after only a fraction of the time spent together? How can I know what to do? My head is telling me to just stop messaging, but my heart is telling me something completely different. I feel as if I left a piece of me with Sebastian. I'm not myself anymore; here I'm still Anthony's wife, and a part of this house, but in Italy I found the real me again. Sebastian saved me. I know he loves … ahh damn it! What the fuck am I getting myself into Fran?"

Francesca topped off my glass. "Let it out baby girl," she said reassuringly. "Do you want to know what I think? Here it is in a nut shell. Sometimes it feels as though Anthony loves you for the Julia he met and married. For the woman you were then, and will always be to him, rather than the woman you are now."

I silently sobbed, replying, "Exactly. And if I think back to when we first met … god! I remember how he looked at me, how he spoke to me, and every single time I remember those first few years, I love him all the more. I don't know, Fran. I don't know. I don't know whether we work together anymore. What if we keep fighting with each other instead of for each other? What if we just can't make each other happy anymore?"

My friend, my wonderful confidant, stared at the vase of roses on the side table that Anthony had given to me the night before and carefully pulled one out.

"As you say, you and Anthony have been through a lot. Do you think you would be just as happy with Sebastian in a few years as you are now? At the beginning, it's difficult; you only see the best of each other. It's all rosy, right Jules? But you know as well as I do there are no roses without thorns. Think about what you're bringing into your world. Can you handle it? Do you know who he really is?"

"Of course I do. I know he would never hurt me. But you think I should stop things with him before I get in too deep, don't you?"

"Ah, baby girl, I think you already are in deep shit, if you pardon my French! I love you Jules, and I am sorry but you need to hear the truth. You want to justify this distorted relationship with Sebastian and try to rationalize why you love him, rather than accepting the truth from your intuition shouting at you to let him go. I think you should listen to your gut and let it all go. The truth is that this could never have turned out any different, because maybe, it was meant to be temporary. Jules my dearest friend, only you can create your own happiness, and I want you to be happy. Whatever choices you make, I'll respect them, and I'll always be here for you."

"I love you Fran. You may be right, but I can't seem to let him go, and I don't know why? How will I know?" I asked desperately. "How will I ever know the decision to make?"

Fran poured the last bit of prosecco into our glasses, put the bottle down, and gently held my hand.

"When the time is right, you will just instinctively know what to do, what your heart leads you to do." She squeezed my fingers. What her being there meant to me in that moment, well, it went beyond words.

"Enough about me ..." I sighed, wanting to talk about something new to get off this topic so that we could go back to smiling, laughing even. "How are things with your beau? You missing him yet?"

"Like I'd miss my favorite lipstick." She pouted, only half in jest. Fran and Alessandro had met in Italy, on the same trip where I had met Sebastian. She had immediately fallen head over heels, despite her claims that she was only searching for a summer fling. They had stayed in contact since, but I knew that the distance was hard.

"When did you guys speak last?" I asked.

"Ummmm," Fran finished her spoonful of gelato. "Day before yesterday. He's doing good, busy with work. He's been babysitting his niece a lot as well, so our conversations lately have been a little short and primarily about diapers and baby stuff. Jesus, we better get some 'us' time soon, you know?"

Fran smirked, and I laughed. She would often make jokes in lieu of expressing difficult emotions; over the years I had learned when to let things go, and when to push further.

"You can always come over if you need to rant," I reminded her. "I like not being the only hopeless case."

"Oh sweetie," Francesca said, grinning. "Who said anything about a hopeless case? Both of us can kick some butt if we have to. Anyways, our stories give us character and personality. So, I'd say we're hopeless romantics. I like that better."

"Yes, me too. Now let's finish what we started," I replied, gesturing to the tub of gelato. "I still prefer to eat my sorrows away."

"No!" she declared. "Once you're done sulking, you go put on those Jimmy Choos. They have no added calories and you're totally badass when you wear them."

I couldn't help but believe her. Everything was slightly better with the right pair of shoes. Leave it to Fran to always make me laugh.

★ ★ ★

Fran was right—time would tell me what I needed to know, and my heart would lead me to where I was meant to be. Maybe then I would see clearly concerning Sebastian. I prayed and wrote and cried for a sign, and it didn't seem to help me, as none came.

Which is how I ended up cleaning my kitchen in a frenzy, consciously waiting for my phone to vibrate. I desperately wanted to have the message come through. Maybe he had changed his mind. Maybe he wouldn't come …

After what seemed like hours, my phone finally lit up on the countertop. I dove for it.

```
My darling Julia! Everything has been
arranged. I'm just about to take off. Every
moment of this flight is a moment where I'm
closer to you. See you soon, amore mio.
Ti amo.
```

I sighed, pressing the phone to my lips. It was happening. Sebastian was actually moving to Canada to be with me.

I stopped cleaning and made my way upstairs. I had begun my journal at the start of my meeting Sebastian, and it only seemed fitting to continue keeping it. The journal held all of my secret life, emotions, and thoughts about our encounters, even some of our text messages, writing them down so that I wouldn't forget them when at some point they would be deleted from my phone. Words and poems—those that he sent—were precious to me.

The texts had started out so desperate, and gradually became so much more intimate. From the first to the last, my heart broke as I read them. How could I have such a wonderful and romantic man fall in love with me, now, at this point in my life? He had loved me for what felt like forever. How could I ever tell him not to come …?

```
Julia, I just watched your plane leave,
and I can't believe you're really gone.
I can't tell you how much I desire you to
turn around and come back to me. You have
made your choice, I know, but I'm not sure
if you know mine. My choice is to fight for
you. We belong together, my love, and I'll
adore you through this lifetime and into
the next. Even if I can never have you as
my own, know that my thoughts are of you.
Mind, body, and soul.
```

He had missed me so, and he hadn't known just how much I missed him. I didn't tell him that I had lain my head against the plane window, tears pouring out of my eyes the entire flight home. I knew, though, that being strong was important, or at least faking strength. The truth was, I hadn't known what I wanted then. I only knew what I thought was "right."

I had tried so hard at first to keep Sebastian and his messages at bay. Soon, though, my strength began to wane, and he had been able to sense it …

I LOVE YOU STILL

```
Do you miss me, my darling? Despite the
long time apart, every time I step into
my bedroom I'm transported back to where
we were. You have messed with my reality,
my love, and you will forever own me. The
open window won't remove the smell of
your perfume, nor my memories of how we
would talk for hours after making love. I
miss waking up to feel you in my arms and
begin the day as one. Until we meet again
- Sebastian
```

With every message I had felt his lips on mine, his hands stroking my back. I had been thrown into the abyss of need and pleasure and found myself entirely unable to resurface. He intoxicated me with his words and totally satisfied me without laying a hand on my body. Every day we were apart only brought us closer together. What began as a pang of longing and uncertainty quickly became a whirlwind of emotion. This man, who I believed was my soulmate, had a part of my heart. I couldn't resist him. And still, history has shown that fully opening your heart to forbidden love can sometimes come at a cost. But I hadn't cared. My heart wanted what Sebastian offered me.

I had been the one to encourage him to come close to me. I wanted to see him in my world, in Canada. And I knew what would happen when I did.

★ ★ ★

The drive to his new apartment was agony. Overwhelmed by confusion, I questioned whether he should even be there at all.

Sebastian told me from the start that he would never force me to do anything I wasn't comfortable with. All he asked of me was time. Time to see me and talk without an ocean between us. My heart was racing as I got closer to his condo. All of a sudden, I found it hard to breathe.

Calm down. He's come all this way, so the least you can do is see that he's alright. If nothing else. Right. Who was I trying to convince?

I paused outside of the tall, modern building, the traffic around me and bustle of well-dressed businessmen blurring my mind and increasing my anxiety. What if someone were to see me here and mention it to Anthony? But then again, who would know? I was merely visiting a friend.

I held my breath as I entered the foyer of the building. A porter sat inside watching me as I waited. I greeted the man. He asked me who I was and who I wanted to visit. I frowned, my heart pounding. I hadn't expected to give my name. The building was of course of high caliber, and it made sense that they would want to keep track of who entered and left. I sighed.

"I'm here to see Mr. DeLuca," I replied, and quickly signed my name with a flourish. Emilia DeLuca.

He smiled and buzzed Sebastian before pressing the button for me to enter. "Go on up Mrs. DeLuca."

I frowned, and yet did so with a pounding heart. I hadn't expected that. I wasn't sure why I had chosen that name, or why I affiliated myself to Sebastian in that way. What if someone were to find out? And yet, it made sense to me. There, in Sebastian's world, I needed to feel as if I belonged.

Never had an elevator journey felt so long. Thoughts rushed through me as I ruffled my hair in the mirror and touched up my lipstick. I was supposed to be faithful to Anthony; why was I doing this? Did I want something more to happen?

Yes, I did. But I also knew I shouldn't.

His door was already open when I exited the elevator. His condo was stunning. There he was, waiting for me, his feet bare and sleeves rolled up. The top button of his shirt was undone, and he wore it with impeccably tailored trousers and a Gucci belt. Subtle, tasteful, effortlessly elegant, and still slightly casual. He looked as though he had just left a meeting and was ready to welcome me home.

"Sebastian," I whispered, rushing to him. My bag hit the floor, as my arms wrapped around his shoulders. Tears came swiftly; he lifted me up, holding me tightly. I squeezed him, our desire to be as close as possible with our clothes between us.

"I've missed you so much," I confessed. "I can't believe you're really here!"

He buried his face in my hair, and I could feel his warm breath against my ear as he let out a long sigh of relief. God, he smelled so good.

"Every moment apart was a moment I was missing a part of myself," he murmured. "With a love that the winged seraphs of Heaven, coveted you and me …"

"That's beautiful."

He placed me gently on my feet and kissed my forehead.

"It's Edgar Allan Poe," he said.

I had always envisioned the works of Poe as being within the genre of the Gothic and macabre. And yet … such wonderful proclamations of love. Sebastian placed his hand on the small of my back to guide me into the living room.

"Would you like some wine, my love?" he asked.

"Please." He knew exactly how to calm me. "How was your flight? I'm sorry I wasn't there to pick you up ... wow, this is a beautiful place. How did you find it?"

I settled myself on his sofa and took in the surroundings as he went to fetch a bottle. The interior was every bit as sophisticated as I had expected. The grey of the large sofa paired well with the wooden furnishings and cream carpet—a vibe of masculine elegance. I smiled at the large, ornate bookshelf that dominated the room. A large portion was filled with poetry, and flutters ran through me at the memories of his words. The cadence, the intonation, the exquisite meaning professed from his soft lips with his smooth voice. His accent tended to have a slight rasp when he'd had some whisky. Reading to me, Sebastian brought something different to my life.

He returned with two glasses of wine and said, "So many questions my love, and you know why I didn't want you at the airport? It would have been too dangerous for you. And as for my new home, money can get you anything these days amore."

"You're right. I was even worried about coming here. And, by the way, I'm now Emilia DeLuca to your doorman. This place is so you. How are you settling in?"

"Much better now that you're here Emilia." His eyes, though, were sorrowful. "I hope you like what I chose? How long are you able to stay?"

Forever, I thought.

"I love it Sebastian, especially your library. I can stay until seven or so," I said.

He reached for the decanter and poured more wine into each glass. With a blush, I raised my glass to his, clinking them gently together.

"Welcome to Canada," I said.

He replied with, "To us, my love."

We each took a sip, and then set our glasses down. I wanted him to kiss me at that moment, and yet I knew that a kiss wouldn't be enough. He took my lips into his. My head spun, and I felt like I was home again. Sebastian, I knew, felt the same.

MONTAUK

The art of writing is the art of discovering what you believe.

Gustave Flaubert

Present

The sun was already starting to rise when I gave up on sleeping entirely. My husband lay beside me, his expression soft, eyelashes long against his cheeks and mouth sweetly parted. The luminescent glow coming in through our window made him seem almost angelic. He appeared innocent, perfect in sleep. If only that were true …

In that moment, I could only see him as he was: a beautiful and flawed human being. I moved slowly, determined not to wake him. I unlocked our door and headed to the place I loved the most. Sitting cross-legged and watching the ocean, I began to write.

My Darling Anthony,

I LOVE YOU STILL

Words can't express how sorry I am for what I have done to you, and how pained I am by what you have done for me. Guilt rips me apart every moment I'm unable to confess to you the truth.

I love you, Anthony, I truly do. I love you so much that my heart aches, that I feel sorrow instead of jealousy each time you are home late, or your phone is turned off. I cry for you, Anthony. I cry for the memories of our young, carefree joy. But I realize that in this life, in this relationship that we have built together, there is no way for us to go back. I'm not even sure whether there is a way in which we can move forward.

Sometimes I fight with what my heart wants and what my mind knows. I long to remember the love we had. We have had such a wonderful journey. At times it's been unpleasant and underwhelming, but all marriages are. I love to think of those moments that we were able to grow and fight for each other. You, Tony, are the choice that I made so long ago, and the choice that I intended to stand by for the rest of my life. Even if I have failed you, I'm committed to you in a way that I would never be able to commit to anyone else.

The only string pulling me away from you is my lover, a man I realize is now a part of me. I don't think you would be able to truly accept that I never intentionally looked to fall in love with another man … but I did. You wouldn't be able to come to terms with my betrayal, or the life that I have lived with this man, right under your nose, at times even in our home. I have tainted what was once our sacred space, and yet I tricked my mind into thinking I deserved it. He is as different from you as night is from day, and yet he is so in tune with me that I can only think it's because we were destined. I was meant to meet him even if it meant my destruction.

While, yes, our love will constantly change and shift with time and circumstance, I fear that my love for Sebastian will always be there. My discovery of him was a discovery of myself in many ways. It's who I have now become. I have worked so hard to find myself and yet I can't say at times I like who I am.

Sebastian has allowed me to be flawed and imperfect. Needless to say, I'm not the same woman I was when we first met. I'm more real, freer. I only wish that you would be able to love me still as I am right now, after finding out about this secret that I kept from you.

Have you not noticed the change in me, my husband? Have you not seen the darkness in my world, the fierce energy that has fueled me in the last year? I suppose you haven't. But then again, I also haven't felt, seen, or understood what's happening in your life anymore. We are simply two separate people, living the same life, existing in the same home. Now I shall try to understand you, as Sebastian understands me.

I have never truly believed in fate as I do now. Fate took us apart, and fate took me to him. Maybe we can find true happiness again now that I choose to make you my priority. But how will you not be able to see the chaos inside of me? I will always long for him … I will never truly be that bright light for you, not while I'm without my whole heart, but I will try, for you I will TRY! I can only pray that you will still love me the same and know that I will always love you.

Julia

★ ★ ★

I sighed and stood, holding the paper in my hands. The rising sun was hitting the sand and water; it was sapphire-like. The breeze brushed through my hair, whipping it around my face and cleansing my skin with its cool kiss. I closed my eyes, letting the serenity wash over me. In that moment, I was alone with the ocean.

When I returned to myself and set the paper afire, allowing the ashes to fall and christen this place that I loved, the waves drew higher once more, crashing against rocks and smoothing away the marks of early morning dog walkers. Everything was now as it should be. A clean slate.

WHITE SHEETS, CANADA

To think of him in the middle of the day lifts me out of ordinary living.

Anais Nin

One week earlier

Sebastian pressed me back against the stone wall. His lips brushed against my ear and it brought a quiet moan, and I shivered.

"Spread your legs my love," he whispered. I stepped both feet apart as I watched him looking at me. "Keep your back against the wall, and don't move."

I walked my feet out further and it felt as if my legs would fail me if he hadn't had his hips pressed against mine. The anticipation alone of what he would do next caused my breathing to intensify, and he hadn't even touched me yet.

I LOVE YOU STILL

"My love," he murmured huskily. "I know you're wet. I could make you experience such intense pleasure without even a touch. I own you, all of you." He smiled at me, the small seductive quirk of his lips weakening me. "Tell me, my love, what do you want me to do to you?"

He had hiked up my dress, and was slowly running his hand along my thigh, still pressing up against me. His eyes were fiery, and I couldn't help but let out another small whimper at the pleasure that shot through me when he finally pushed my panties aside and slipped his fingers inside of me, controlling me with such sensual strokes. I knew I wouldn't last long, and my mind couldn't process anything but the sensation of him against me, the smell of our arousal, and the sounds of our heavy breathing.

"Ahh, so wet," he crooned. "I can smell your passion; I know what you want." His one hand played with me, while the other pushed my black lace bra aside. He used his tongue and lips to encircle my erect nipples, biting and licking softly, only lifting his head to look me straight in the eyes and whisper, "You know I'll always own you, my love?"

"Yes," I whimpered, my eyes closing as he used his mouth to tip my chin, keeping his face level with mine, my gaze now focused on his dark intensity. He rubbed me in precise circles, building higher and higher ... I matched my lover's strokes with my body. Gripping him tightly and digging my fingers into his shoulders, I finally let the intense pleasure overtake me, screaming out his name as I exploded. "Sebastian! Oh god! Yes, yes ... ohhh, fuck!"

With a long moan, my body dissolved and collapsed into his. His touch, the lust, the orgasm he had just given me, was of such an erotic and sinful intensity ... unfamiliar. It wasn't just the sex or the excitement; it was the matching of minds, of needs, of appetites. He knew from when he first saw me that I would always be his; that he could draw from me the wild creature that nobody else could.

He pressed me tighter against him and growled possessively, "Surely you don't think that I'm done with you yet, my love? I want you to feel my touch burning on your skin for days. I want you to remember my fingers trailing up your thighs as you walk tomorrow. I want you to see your beautiful flushed face each time you look in the mirror and remember your orgasms. My wild creature, I want you to remember that you're mine."

His hardness rubbed against my tingling skin, and his hips jerked as I anxiously reached for his belt buckle. His lips found my throat, his breath and kisses hot, slow … soft, and teasing.

"What is it that you want, Julia?"

I want everything, I longed to scream, but I couldn't find the words. I was consumed by my desperate desire for him. I shook my head and leaned forward to press my lips against his. He laughed softly and pulled his head back as my breathing quickened and my body began to shake.

"My love," he teased. "I need you to tell me."

He was dominant, direct, his actions coming straight out of my fantasies. He knew, of course, that I loved what he was doing to me, but he had never before made me beg. I looked at his rugged, beautiful face.

"Make love to me, Sebastian!" I cried desperately. "Please!"

I was at the brink of ecstasy again, and in desperate need of his body. Cupping his face, I brought his lips to mine. A meeting of wills, I knew that we were made of the same cloth; that we were lovers doomed and meant for only each other.

"Sebastian please, please, I want you now," I begged, feeling my throat tighten with the force of my need. He unzipped my already torn dress to get it off me and carried me to his bedroom.

★ ★ ★

In semi darkness, we had collapsed onto his bed, both of us tangled in the white sheets. He propped himself up on his elbows, his hair mussed and arms strong as he looked tenderly down at me. I felt desired, sensual, and free. I smiled happily at his soft expression. Love had clouded over the previously determined look of lust in his eyes. I reached up to stroke his face, adoring the feel of his cheekbones. His chest rumbled with pleasure.

"I'm desperate for you, Julia; my cravings for you will never be satisfied. To be apart from you is torture. To not see you in my villa, dressed only in my shirt. To not be able to read to you as your head lies on my lap. To lie in bed without your hair in my face … you mean more to me than I can truly say. You're like the moon to me. You come to me in darkness when it's only our world. Our love is like a dream, the most beautiful dream, amore mio."

I kissed his chest and trailed my fingers across the arm that held me close, our bodies still intertwined and drenched from our lovemaking. I remained silent and had to turn away, overcome with sadness for a moment. I wrapped myself in the sheet and walked over to the window. The moon was full that night. The light came right into Sebastian's bedroom. He said I was his moon. How could he speak of me with such adoration?

His eyes followed my every move. He got up and put on his play list. He knew how much I loved his music. I soon felt him behind me. He put his hands on my hips and drew me into him. I began to sway, feeling the song. Sebastian moved with me, spinning me in a small circle before returning to our gentle rocking, with his bare chest against my back. He pulled my head back.

"Who are you?" he whispered.

I felt his strong, hard body against my hips as I turned to face him. He gently pulled me down to the floor, kissing me with a desperate moan. I pretended to wrestle with him, only to get up and stand over him. The moonlight now outlined my curves through the white sheet. I met his eyes with the same hunger and slowly let the sheet drop. I stood still with my legs spread apart like he had demanded of me a few hours ago. I knew he could see how ready I was for him. He grabbed me with such force that I couldn't resist his strength as he pulled me down over his face.

I let out a surprised cry, my knees hitting the floor, and his tongue expertly caressing my sensitive clit. He worshipped me. I couldn't help the small movements of my hips against his talented swipes and the gentle grazes of his teeth against me. My pleasure came quickly and fiercely, and in utter gratitude I screamed out his name. I knew that whatever we were, we would never have enough of each other. I was powerless over my rapture, and that scared me.

His question lingered. *Who are you, Julia? Who have you become?*

★ ★ ★

Lying in his arms, I lost sight of the time. I wanted to talk to him about everything. There was nothing worth keeping from him, and yet how could I tell him about my getaway with Anthony tomorrow? My commitment to my husband weighed heavily on him, and it hurt me to see the expression on his face whenever the topic came up.

He always told me that our love was worth this, and our faith would carry us through. Every time he said so, however, the desperation in his voice grew. I questioned the sanity of our secret life together. In these moments after we made love, I would always find out something new about Sebastian. He seemed more open to share details of his very private life.

"I have some questions, Sebastian."

"Of course, love, questions," he sighed. "Every day you ask questions. Okay, what is it today?"

"Well, sorry but I need to know more about this man that I'm doing unimaginable things with and lying naked beside."

"Are you complaining my love?"

"That would be an affirmative no! You, my lover, drive me crazy in all ways. God, my body is still tingling. Okay, so my first question is … about your mother. You don't talk about her much. What kind of woman is she?"

I took a deep breath, preparing for his answer. His eyes always darkened with the mention of his mother, as he always skirted around the topic. Hopefully, he would understand—I needed to know his past just as well as his present. We had discussed his ex-wife and his daughter, yet we had never talked about his mother.

"She wasn't a mother; I like to think of her as an outlet to my birth." Sebastian rolled away from me. I knew this subject wasn't easy for him. He stared at the ceiling in contemplation.

Finally, he sighed and told me that the beautiful woman who delivered the envelopes last summer to the villa was indeed his mother. Sebastian only referred to his mom by her first name, Daniela. Given his reluctance to talk about her, I wasn't surprised.

"Why did she send you to boarding school at the age of ten?" I asked.

"She didn't want a child in the way. My Zio Marcello, my father's brother, who is very wealthy, organized to send me to a school in France. He wanted his brother's only son to be well educated, and after my father's death, my mother couldn't cope with having to raise a child."

"What happened to your father?" I asked timidly. Aged ten he had already lost his dad, and apparently, for the most part, his mother as well.

"I was very young, but I remember my father well. To me he was like a superhero. He had a thing for wine and took pride in making it. Sometimes in the early mornings he would take me with him into the vineyards to watch the sunrise. He would say to me, 'My son, making wine is like life; you must have love and patience for it. Wine can't be rushed; beautiful things take time, just like the sun rising and setting.'"

I could hear the wistfulness in his tone. It made me want to hold him close to me, but he hadn't answered my question, and this time I wouldn't let it go.

"How did he die, Sebastian?"

His voice cracked, and I almost relented; however, it seemed as important for him to talk about as it was for me to hear it. I squeezed his hand and kissed his jaw.

"He was murdered. I was told that it was a robbery that went wrong. My whole world changed the day my father died.

Zio Marcello took me under his wing and ensured that both my mother and I would never want for anything in life."

"Your Zio Marcello sounds like a good man," I said softly. "Much like you are."

His eyes still bore the weight of his hurt, but his lips smiled; for now, for his sake, I wouldn't ask anymore.

★ ★ ★

Hours of conversation had passed, and we were still cuddled close, spooning in a wonderfully comfortable way. I held his hand between my own, playing with his fingers. He pressed a kiss to the back of my neck, and I felt his lips curl into a smile.

"My love, do you remember that day that you came out in your white dress in Verona? Do you know I wasn't scheduled to drive that day?"

"Yes, I remember it vividly. I felt like a schoolgirl, wondering whether you would like my dress, my hair. I wanted to look good for you. That was the day my life changed."

It was true. I had thought back to that day often, rejoicing in the memory of how he made me feel soft and romantic, and alive. It felt like the moment in a movie when the hero sees the heroine for the first time, and immediately they know it's love.

"You didn't know this," he responded, "but that day, I was walking behind you and watched you so intensely. I admired the outline of your figure as you walked in that white dress … mmm," he purred in my ear, and I felt my body start to respond to him once more. "I wondered whether you wore it on purpose to catch my attention. My heart raced as I imagined myself grabbing your hips and wrapping your beautiful legs around my waist. That was the day I knew without a doubt that I needed to have you. And eventually … well, you know how the rest of this story goes, don't you my love?"

"Sebastian! You're so bad," I teased. "And I may or may not have known that the dress was see-through." He grabbed me and pinned me down and started to kiss me in a way that only led to us being tangled in the sheets again. I looked at the time and realized I couldn't stay much longer.

"Sebastian I can't. I have to leave very soon." I knew after our time together that I couldn't tell him about my weekend in Montauk with Anthony; I didn't want to ruin the moment. All I wanted was to make love to Sebastian once more before I had to go home.

Yet instead, even though I knew I shouldn't, I remained with him for a bit more, curled tighter together.

Sebastian reached for a book that had a silver bookmark inside. "Shall we read, my Beatrice?"

"Beatrice?" I asked, giggling.

"Yes, amore. My salvation."

He opened the book that we had started reading back in Italy and began where we had left off. Dante Alighieri's words now filled with life and meaning. I knew then that the memory of that day would stay forever in my mind.

What I didn't know, and could never have ever predicted, was that it would be the last day I would see him in Canada.

FORGET-ME-NOT

Anyone who has lost something they thought was theirs forever, finally comes to realize that nothing really belongs to them.

Paulo Coelho

Present

You will never have another love story like ours. I told you once that when you start to miss me, remember I didn't let you go. You walked away from me and took my heart with you.

I didn't know what or why this was happening to me, nor would I have been able to explain it to anyone else. My life had spun out of control and you left me wondering why? I accepted the lies to avoid believing the truth. You broke us when you walked away, and you left me with the broken pieces. I don't know if I can forgive you for that. Did you know that, there were times when I wanted desperately to leave you myself, but I couldn't envision any my life without you, and there were times when I wanted nothing more than to stay and never leave you. There were times when I wanted you to leave me, and times when I begged you not to. There were times when I walked out unable to take anymore, and then waited desperately for you to contact me and inevitably draw me back into our crazy love affair. Knowing the truth but believing the lie would most likely be my demise. But I didn't care anymore, as long as you stayed. As long as you loved me forever.

Julia

★ ★ ★

I avoided his emails for a few months after he left. I was mad, hurt, and still trying to convince myself this was for the best. Sebastian leaving meant that I could concentrate on my life now, maybe even piece it back together. My heart had been crushed when I read the message of his decision to return home. Would Sebastian ever understand how much of me belonged to him?

I blamed Sebastian for the mess that was now my life. He had abandoned me when I was in Montauk. I was thus unable to see him, argue with him, gain any form of closure. Truth be told, I wanted him in my life at any cost, and I felt robbed of an opportunity to convince him to stay.

And then there was the day I came to a decision to get answers … Francesca was coming to pick me up, as we were heading to Toronto to meet the girls for lunch and begin planning our Italian getaway. I had been looking forward to it and looking forward to the drive as well. Lovely Fran, the only person that I could entirely trust. I could talk to her about anything. She was the only one who knew about Sebastian.

I slid into the passenger seat and leaned over to kiss her cheek. She smiled and reached for a hug.

"How are you, bella?" she asked as she shifted her foot on the clutch. Straight away she gave me a knowing look, and I could have almost cried out with relief.

"I'm okay Fran," I offered. "Really, I could be much worse. I'm so glad I've got you to talk to."

Francesca turned onto the main road and then reached over to squeeze my hand. "You can always talk to me, Julia. Always."

Just one of the reasons why she was so precious to me. I took a deep breath and lowered the window a notch. The fresh air hit my cheeks; it felt really good.

"I haven't responded to any of his emails yet," I told her. "He hurt me so much by leaving."

"I'm assuming you mean Sebastian?"

"Yes, Fran."

She let out a sigh but shot me a sympathetic look.

"Jules, did you ever stop to think that maybe the person you fell in love with isn't real?" she said gently. "I've been thinking that maybe he could have been an illusion you created. He saw the good in you, validated your insecurities, and he may have taken advantage of your vulnerability. I'm just saying that maybe what you had with him is what you yourself created."

It made no sense. How could I wrap my head around such an idea? No one saw the Sebastian I saw, the one that was so adoring and so open about everything. The one who would send me a good morning text that brought me to life more than my coffee did. The one who would pull me in close for a last embrace not wanting to let go. The one who would read poetry to me, who stopped his life in Italy so he could spend time here with me.

"Why would he want to hurt me? I'm not innocent here either Fran."

"Jules, you let him in," she started. "You said he was your soul mate."

"I thought he was," I whispered. He still was, surely? I sighed. "He told me the same. At times he seemed to know me better than Anthony. He listened to every word I spoke, and always gave me the attention I craved. Was I stupid to believe all that he told me? I just don't understand how he could open up to me like he hadn't before, on the last night we were together, and then just leave, just like that. He made me happy, Fran, he really did. God, I may be devoted to Anthony, but I love Sebastian, I do; he has my heart."

"You're not stupid," she replied sternly. "You were vulnerable. Your relationship with Anthony had you hanging by a thread, and you needed to believe in the goodness of a man again. You want to know what I think? Sebastian saw you as damaged, no offence, and that drew him to you. I also think he was damaged too. Maybe you both thought it was love, but maybe it was something else. Maybe he needed nurturing, and you were the one to give it to him."

I felt my eyes watering and looked away. Had he just seen me as a convenient lover, as the glue that he could use to put himself back together? Maybe he felt as if he was finally fixed and used my devotion to my husband as an excuse to leave me.

"Jules, look at me," Francesca ordered as she stopped at a red light. "Honey listen to me. Sebastian was in control of you the moment he smiled at you and you smiled back; you immediately let him in. You both became what the other one needed; he helped you forget your problems with Anthony, and I get that, I do. But honey, it was only supposed to be temporary, a warm body to get you through your shit, not a forever relationship. Jules, what is it that you think you owe him? Why do you feel so confused?"

"I just want to stop hurting!" I cried. "I don't know how to be me without him; I want the ache gone from my heart. Sebastian's leaving has broken me into more pieces than I was in before we met. This may be the price that I have to pay for what I've done. I feel as if I'm being punished. I never thought I would be here at this point in my life." I squeezed my eyes shut and continued, softer. "I can't hate him; I hate myself for loving him still, and this is all my fault. I molded myself to him so easily and offered him a way into my life. I'm old enough, and I thought wise enough to know this was wrong on so many levels. And yet I still threw away everything to become lost in the experience of this man, my lover. But dammit Fran! You know what? You're so right, his damn smile that day we met, it captured me completely, he ruined me."

"No one should be punished for love, Jules, but this love was unrealistic. You fabricated it together; you were both desperate enough for love, or what you thought was love. You created another life, you created another you, and stayed safe within the world that you both built."

"You're wrong," I argued. "Our love was very real; there's no way that he could have pretended. He loves me, and I love him. Yes, it was unbridled and passionate, but it was love. He's gone away to forget me … I know it and I don't want our world to end."

Fran laughed and gave me that knowing, twinkling smile.

"Well my friend, if that's how you feel, then you're fucked. You know you're going to have to figure this shit out, but for god's sake Jules, my advice would be to forget him and just remember the memories … that's it."

I wanted to reach into my purse to grab my cell, but I froze. I would reach out to him. This man had meant so much to me for so long. Even Fran's warning wouldn't deter me; if anything, it made me realize how much I wanted him back. I wanted nothing more than to hear his voice. He was likely in as much agony as I was, and knowing Sebastian, he would probably be pissed with me for not answering his emails.

Fran shook her head and said, "Message him. Obviously, I know that's what you really want to do, so do it. One thing I've always admired about you, Jules, is that you make sure you learn the lesson no matter the consequences, and this one isn't over yet."

"I'm sorry. I don't know why, but I still need answers from him. Maybe I'll even get closure." I gathered my courage and began typing with shaky fingers. Start simple …

```
Ciao, Sebastian.
```

★ ★ ★

We entered the restaurant and the girls were seated, wine already on the table. Our crazy conversations started to flow. It had been a long time since we had all been together; plus, we needed to organize our upcoming trip. The plan was to travel to Ireland and Italy. Francesca and I were turning fifty, and that's where we wanted to go. Obviously, Italy was my choice, but Fran insisted on a few days in Ireland before that, so we decided to do both.

"Mmmm, I love the idea of some Irish shenanigans with you ladies," I sighed. It was so nice to see everyone, and to plan something fun for a change. With our separate family commitments, time as a group was something that I definitely cherished.

"So, tell me why Christy isn't coming on this trip," Sophia asked.

"She promised her son and daughter-in-law that she would watch the twins this summer," Fran responded, as she stood in dramatic fashion and lifted her glass high. "She will be missed. Before we get started ladies, let's have a toast to friendship, sisterhood, and new adventures. *Slainte* bitches!"

We couldn't help but laugh at her as we raised our own glasses. Fran always knew how to get things started.

"Isn't it slan-ta?" I asked.

"Honestly, Jules, I'm going to smack you. We're going to Ireland, so get it right already," Filomena said.

I shook my head and grinned, certain that this would become a running joke during our upcoming trip. We quickly dove into planning our holiday. I imagined it would be weird now … to be in the place where I had met Sebastian, while so acutely grieving the loss of him.

Fran would be staying in Italy for a while longer—her rendezvous with Alessandro awaited. While I traveled to Ravello to meet up with Anthony, she would be with Alessandro, a man she had met on one of our previous girls' trips. They would be coming back to Canada together a couple of days later, and I knew that Fran was even considering introducing him to her kids—a huge step.

Despite her looking for just a fun, light-hearted "holiday fling" at the time, she and Alessandro really connected and had stayed in contact. This didn't edit Alexandra's planning, but she had seemed to take it as an excuse to plan even more intricately than usual. My sister Alexandra was always the reason why our trips went smoothly—while the rest of us came up with ideas, she connected all the dots into a neatly organized itinerary that made the trip itself incredibly enjoyable.

Sophia, my younger sister, popped into the conversation quite quickly before our party planner could get into the full swing of things. "I don't know how I'm going to manage leaving on June 29; that's the day after the girls finish school."

"You have done this before," Alexandra responded calmly. "Just make sure you have everything in order, and Bobby will take care of it as he always does."

I grinned, knowing that my wonderful sister Sophia would be worrying about her family every moment until we arrived at our destination. "I'll have my meds ready for the plane ride, just in case you need them sis," I said.

"I think I'm good," Sophia replied. "Remember how they knocked me out on the last trip we took? Hmmm, on second thoughts, yes, please bring them just in case."

"Since I'm in charge of transportation, should I send Sebastian an email to ask if he's available?" Filomena asked.

"He took such good care of us the last time we were there," I said, trying to sound casual, but my friends seemed to know better. While they weren't aware of what had happened in Canada, they had been there when I met him in Italy and had seen the spark between us. He had driven us around, showing us the sights while engaging us in wonderfully stimulating conversation. Most of the time it was me he was staring at as he spoke. They knew of my decision to stay back with him. The choice to remain behind wasn't received well. Alexandra tried desperately to change my mind. My sisters never knew how involved I had gotten with Sebastian. They didn't ask and I didn't tell. I always felt that they wouldn't understand.

Alexandra, always protective of me, smoothly intervened. "Why don't we drive? It would be another experience to add to our list."

"Who is going to drive those crazy roads in Italy?" Filomena asked.

"Yes who?" I desperately added.

"I will," Fran cried out excitedly.

"Oh god. We're going to die!" Filomena gasped as she threw her hands in the air in defeat. There was no way in hell any of us would get behind the wheel in such unfamiliar terrain, and I knew that Filomena and Sophia would be with me on that. Alexandra might give it a try, but she would stay well below the speed limit. So, we decided to put our lives in Fran's hands.

We all exploded once more into giddy, uncontrollable laughter. We definitely got the attention of the other guests in the restaurant. Some were amused by our antics, but others clearly less so. It didn't matter—we made our own entertainment. It was during this moment that I felt my phone vibrate. My thoughts immediately returned to Sebastian, and I excused myself for the washroom; I had to read the message.

```
Finally, amore, you have made me wait so
long. How are you?

I'm fine.
```

I told myself: *Play it cool, Julia.*

```
Every man knows that when a woman says fine,
it's not a good thing.
```

I felt irritated. Did he want to launch immediately into an argument? Why couldn't we enjoy a little small talk first?

```
Well what do you want me to say?
```

I sighed, my phone pinging again almost the moment that I locked the screen. I needed time to think.

```
The truth, Julia! Just the truth.
```

I felt tears begin to sting my eyes. I was angry and hurt, and so very emotional. I was in a public place. I needed to pretend that everything was okay. I closed my eyes and inhaled deeply, letting the breath out slowly, counting to ten before I returned to his text and replied.

```
I'm mad at you for leaving me.
```

```
I could say the same.
```

How could he be upset with me? I hadn't left him. Did he mean that he was mad at himself? If he regretted his departure, then why hadn't he said so? A few unread emails surely weren't an apology, were they? He had let me linger, trapped in this painstaking world of uncertainty. I hadn't known whether he had left me because he didn't want to love me anymore, or because he had. Regardless, I didn't have time to think everything through clearly. Later, I could manage it, but later.

```
I'm with the girls right now, so I need
to go. Later, please. We really do need
to talk.

FaceTime me? Until then, my love.
```

His love? My heart rose and fell in one confused swoop. And yet, my lover had left me. I realized the time on my way back to the table, and quietly murmured to Fran, "We will have to leave shortly if that's okay. I have my last dress fitting appointment."

She nodded and placed her napkin onto her empty plate, saying excitedly, "I still can't believe my godson is getting married."

"Until next time, ladies. Love you all and I can't wait to celebrate," I said in farewell.

Following a quick round of hugs and promises to get together soon, Francesca and I left. Once we were in the car and had started driving, Fran turned to me with a sly grin. "So, what took you so long in the restroom?"

I glanced nervously down at my lap. "Well, Sebastian responded to my text."

"What did he say?" she asked eagerly. "Was it good?"

"We didn't really get anywhere," I admitted. "He wanted to dive straight into it, but I told him I couldn't. I mean, I can't figure out my life in the women's bathroom! This may take a while. He asked me to FaceTime later today."

"Are you okay with him not driving us this time?"

"I actually think it's better. It would be very awkward."

"I agree girlfriend. It's too dangerous."

Ever the wonderful friend, Fran knew there was nothing left to say; she nodded and changed the conversation to my son Matteo's upcoming nuptials. Adriana, his wife-to-be, was truly wonderful, and I was so excited to see them take this beautiful step together. I had never seen a couple so suited for one another; it made my heart both ache for them and also brim with happiness.

Fran stayed with me during my fitting appointment, cracking jokes with the seamstress who was otherwise busy pinning up the hem. We had shopped there before; in fact, it was our go-to for special occasions. Deborah, a sweet elderly lady with bad joints but a motherly smile, knew both of us from our previous purchases. She asked about my children and ribbed Fran about her ostensibly carefree lifestyle.

We left happy. Strange, given the nervous knots in my stomach regarding my imminent conversation with Sebastian. I promised to pick up the dress in two days.

SEE ME

You loved me — what right did you have to leave me?

Emily Bronte

Missing you is a feeling that I deal with every day.

I miss lying next to you as you read to me. I miss turning to you to laugh at a private joke. I miss sitting in silence after a long day, sipping wine and enjoying the companionship of just being together. I don't just miss you for what you give me or what we do together, I miss you as a limb that's missing from my body. Sometimes I can feel you, as if you are still there, but then I come back to myself and find it was a cruel joke. I don't necessarily miss your eyes or your body, or the way you kiss—I miss the feeling of home in your arms.

Home is truly where the heart is, and my heart is with you.

Julia

★ ★ ★

I had just finished adding the remaining wine to the simmering risotto when my phone rang. It was Anthony; he had promised to be home on time for dinner. The buzzing continued, and I quickly grabbed my phone from the kitchen counter.

"Hi honey," I greeted him, hoping that he was on his way home. I continued stirring the risotto, not wanting it to stick to the pan.

"Hi, Jules. I just wanted to let you know that I'm running a little late. I'm stuck in traffic, and it doesn't look as if it's going to move any time soon."

"Oh," I responded. "Late again, on risotto night no less. Did you just leave the office?"

"I'm sorry. I had to take care of something that couldn't wait. I'll make it up to you. See you soon, okay?"

I forced a happy voice for him. "Sure. Drive safely."

He was always late. While he was home more now than he had been in the past, running late was a continuous issue.

My timer beeped and I pulled out the freshly baked bread. I didn't often have time to bake bread; I had done it because I knew Anthony loved it. I loved it too, but I wouldn't make such an effort in cooking only for myself. I have had many lonely meals, and they were never as fulfilling as having food and a good conversation with my husband.

I turned off the flame on the stove with a sigh and put the lid on the pot. It seemed that I would be waiting, again, for a man. First Sebastian, leaving me in a state of desperate confusion, and now my husband. I knew he worked hard, and I knew the traffic wasn't his fault, but after so many evenings spent eating alone, or nursing my wine as I waited, I couldn't help the bitterness. I was disappointed. I needed, for once, to feel like a priority to someone.

I poured wine from the carafe into my large glass and fidgeted with my phone. Should I just wait, like I always did? I had promised Sebastian that I would FaceTime with him. Before I could talk myself out of it, I pressed the button. He quickly answered, as if he was waiting for me. He looked the same as ever, neatly groomed, breathtakingly handsome.

"Ciao, amore," he greeted me.

"Hi Sebastian, how are you?"

"I'm good. You look so beautiful … and annoyed. Why my love?"

My heartbeat quickened, and I suddenly felt as if I couldn't breathe. He still had such an effect on me and knew my moods. I had phoned him, yes, but it had been so very long since we had last spoken. I hadn't known whether we would ever speak again. Just seeing him was enough to overwhelm me. I had no patience at that moment for small talk; I simply wanted answers.

"Thank you. Ahh Sebastian, do you remember telling me once to take us one day at a time and let love lead us? I want to know the real reason you left without talking to me first. Why?"

"My love, I do remember and that's the truth. But Julia, amore, I have questions too. I've emailed you for months. Why no response? Is it because I have things to say that you don't want to hear?"

He looked sad, I had to admit, but part of me was glad. I was in pain—why shouldn't he suffer the same? He continued.

"You have someone to be with all the time. Coming to Canada was to be with you more, yet I still felt alone. When

I wanted you, you were with him. When I needed you, you were with him. When I wanted to make love to you, you were making love to him."

I flinched. He was right, but also so very wrong. He had known all along that I was married. I had never hidden this from him.

"Sebastian, you knew I was a married woman, and you accepted my life," I replied firmly.

"I did. You're correct Julia, but you asked me why I made the decision to leave. It was made after your decision to not tell me about your weekend away with him. After we made love … twice. How do you think I felt? That night I knew I would only ever have half of you, and I want all of you. Is that hard to understand?"

"Oh Sebastian, I'm sorry I kept that from you. And no, you're wrong. I didn't give you half of me, I gave you all of me. But you need to understand, I have obligations, a family. I had a life before you, and I have a life with you and apart from you. It doesn't make me love you any less. On the contrary, it makes me love you more. And it certainly doesn't stop me from hurting every moment that you're gone."

Sebastian sighed deeply then, and I could see his eyes glistening with the tears. A pang shot through me; I was overwhelmed with desire to comfort him. His pain was my pain—it was so difficult to see him so vulnerable.

"You see, my love," he said, "I always found myself missing you more when I was close to you. I never knew how broken and empty I was until I met you. All I want is to be with you and wake up next to you without you having to run off to him. I want to be your first kiss in the morning and your last before bed. When I think of you with him, my heart shatters and I feel my world slowly collapsing around me. I thought I could handle it, but, my love, I can't. I would be lying to myself if I were to try to run from what we have. But I needed to break away for your sake."

"Can you understand my torment?" I whispered. "I want you and him both, something so impossible, but I still wish for it. I wake up every morning teetering between two realities. Sebastian, I want you to know that I never did it on purpose … not tell you that is. I just didn't know how."

"I knew on our last night together that I didn't want to share you with anyone else. After you left, I couldn't sleep as my bed suddenly felt so big and I felt so alone without you. My thoughts went back to our first kiss. I remember how I tasted sadness on your lips. I wondered whether I was forcing you into something you didn't really want. But then your kiss changed, and I started to taste your desire, a need so deep that I knew in a way I was kissing you back to life …"

I felt a desperation in his words that I had never felt before.

"Ahh, my love," he continued. "You're all I could ever want and need, and yet you're all I can never have. It's you, amore … only you, forever. I've chosen you and there will never be anyone else that I'll give my heart fully to Julia. I'll come back only if you intend to be mine forever … and only then. But we both know that will never happen. Always know this: Ti adoro; mi fai impazzire, e desidero solo te."

His statement seemed so final. *I love you; you drive me crazy, and I just want you*. I sniffed, swallowing down the urge to scream at the unfairness of life. The silence was deafening, and that's probably why I was startled when I heard a car roll into the driveway. *Shit*.

"Oh my god," I rushed out. "He's home. I have to go. I'll call you again soon Sebastian. I love you … still …"

Sebastian appeared defeated at the mention of my husband. Should I apologize for the presence of a man who had been a part of my life for far longer than I had known him? I didn't have to decide. He gave me a sad smile and hung up.

HOME

Perhaps it's completely natural that a woman in love forgets everything else. It's not selfishness, for her thoughts are not of herself but of the ones she loves.

Modesta Tonan

The transparency of my sins is an uncharted passage of time that foregoes all reasoning, for my journey is one of love, deception, and friendship that creates a boundless channel of spiraling pain.

To catch my breath is labored as I seek to find the light of Heaven as my guidance. Guidance in what is otherwise a solitude. For I know that all that I am and all that I am to be is beautiful, yet fragile in my way of thinking, which in turn creates a façade of protection as I tend to slowly barricade everything I knew to be true.

Sometimes painfully, we have all been familiar with the sins of transience as our past inexorably resides with the occurrences of the future. The unfolding chapters of my life are not scripted nor are they written in creed; for the imperfections of who I am are the essence of an imperfect soul.

Julia

★ ★ ★

Anthony came into the house through the mud room just as I was putting my phone away and standing to set the table. He entered the kitchen silently, and I jumped guiltily.

"Tony!" I snapped. "Risotto shouldn't wait. You know it should be eaten straight away, not when you feel like it. It's probably ruined!" I pushed away guilty tears. "You told me you would be home for dinner tonight. That's why I made it. And I baked you bread!"

He looked repentant as he presented me with a bouquet that he had hidden behind his back.

"I'm sorry Jules, you know how it goes. I couldn't get out on time. Too many meetings. And traffic is always bad this time of day. Don't worry. I'll eat it all. I'm starving."

Regardless of his comforting words, his tone was condescending and his excuses old. The flowers were my favorite, roses, the same flowers he brought home every time he wanted to smooth things over. Our quarrels had gotten much worse over the years, more desperate, and full of attempts to hurt each other. I was hurt by his negligence, and he was hurt by losing my constant adoration. We now fought harder, the combination of our love and anger fueling the destructive fire of our marriage. The guilt had become a part of our life, and it saddened me that this was who we were now. Every feeble attempt to repair what we once had only brought us more sorrow when it failed. The behaviors that had once been born of innocent love were now mockeries to placate us in times of disagreement.

I put the flowers in a tall stained-glass vase and neatly arranged them. I did care for the aesthetic, but I was mostly avoiding eye contact with Anthony until I had time to compose myself. Anthony dished up the risotto and poured the white wine I had picked out. One that I knew he loved.

"This is delicious," he said. "Just how my mother used to make it."

I smiled. From Anthony, this was a huge compliment. His mother was precious to him. I reached across the table to squeeze his hand. I knew he missed her.

"I miss her too," I said softly. "She was a wonderful woman."

He smiled back and replied, "She really was. She would have been so happy to see our Matteo get married."

"She would have been making jokes about great grandchildren the moment the marriage was official."

He chuckled. "And straightening everyone's ties. Heaven help you if your collar was out of place."

I giggled. "But she would also be telling the children the most ridiculous tales. Do you remember when she convinced Mia that eating eggplant would make her see unicorns?"

"Yes. She even described the unicorn in great detail and told her that they wandered the heath. Mia offered to walk her dog for weeks."

I took a sip of my wine before asking, "Do you remember the speech she made on our wedding day? It was beautiful."

He nodded sadly. "It's a shame that she won't be doing the same for Matty and Adriana. He deserves a beautiful speech."

"We will have to give him one," I said determinedly. "Everything that his nonnas wished for us, I wish for Matteo. A beautiful family, faith in each other, to experience the many phases of life together."

"The passionate expression, the deeper love that comes from familiarity, the time that we spend caring for each other, the joint venture of raising good children that we can be proud of," Anthony continued. "As we've done with ours."

"We have," I agreed. "They have all grown to be such wonderful people. I'm so, so proud of them."

For all of our faults, we had been good role models for our children, and it was an honor to see them continue to build on the traditions that we had started. I remembered being utterly enamored by Anthony when we first met, drawn to his strength, intelligence, and gentle ways. Well, I was also a sucker for a bad boy, and Anthony was the whole package.

We finished dinner, which was pleasant. For the first time in years, we were more absorbed in talking to each other than consuming our meal. Anthony stood and picked up both our glasses and the bottle of wine.

"Let's go up to bed and start watching *Mad Men* on Netflix, Jules. We always said we wanted to. We can relax and continue our conversation."

"Okay, I'd like that. You go up ahead," I said. "I'll just clean up the kitchen and then come join you."

This gave me the opportunity to send a quick text to Sebastian. He had hung up abruptly earlier, and I was feeling terrible about it. I wanted to say goodnight.

I LOVE YOU STILL

```
I'm sorry Sebastian for having to end our
FaceTime so quickly. Goodnight, and let me
know if you want to talk again … xo?
```

I finished wiping down the surfaces and went upstairs, snuggling up beside Anthony. He wrapped his arms around me and pulled me close. I looked up at him, seeing the set of his jaw, so identical to our son.

"Gosh, Matteo looks so much like you. Do you remember those first few nights when we brought him home from the hospital?" I asked him.

Anthony smiled and squeezed me tight. "Yes. Do you remember his tiny hands and big head with reddish hair? Still not sure where that came from."

I did remember. He was so perfect; he took my breath away every time I looked at him. We had made him together, a gift born of our love for each other.

"He was so gorgeous, even then," I said.

Anthony snorted. "His face was constantly red, and he wouldn't stop farting. But yes, he was absolutely perfect."

"And our daughters. I've always loved how you are with them. You were so protective from the moment they came home with us. You have always shown them so much love and respect; I want them to know the standard to hold their own partners to."

"Jules, a man should always protect and care for his family. If anyone upsets them or hurts them, they know that they can come to us. Always."

At that moment, in Anthony's arms, I was happy—I felt safe. Why wasn't it enough for me? I would never want to hurt him; I had always just wanted to make him happy. Yet I knew I had done things that were dishonest, disloyal, and I had broken our vows. It would kill Anthony if he ever found out. I stopped looking directly into his eyes, fearful that he would be able to see my disloyal thoughts.

He was still smiling at me, thinking of the wonderful family that we had made together. I did love him so. Sometimes I longed for how things were when we first married, when we brought Matteo home, when we raised him and his sisters. Funny how now it seemed as if it was such a carefree time. It was important to both of us that we stayed connected and promised each other that we would never go to bed angry. So many memories and promises of young love.

We would clench our mouths shut when we made love, so we wouldn't wake the children. Sleep deprived, with headaches from the crying, we still couldn't keep our hands off each other. We had needed to be close. Now our home was empty, and we were alone again. Not trying to stay silent, not trying to finish quickly, just trying to stay connected …

Ironically, our love life had improved since my trip to Italy. I had thrown myself back into our relationship. I wanted to be better to my husband. I needed to embrace him, to show him how much he still meant to me.

I reached up and stroked his beard, loving the familiar scratchy sensation and the white hairs that peppered it. My husband, my silver fox, the father of my children. I held his cheek and sat up, leaning over him kissing his soft lips, slightly cracked from the way he chewed on his top lip when stressed out. He let out a small moan as he held my head in place and slowly teased my mouth with his tongue.

"Mmmmm," I breathed into him, gently scraping my teeth over his tongue. The taste of risotto and wine mingled together with the taste of my husband … this was amazingly erotic. He rolled us over so he could cover my body with his own.

"I love you," he whispered. "So, so much Jules. You're my life."

"I love you too."

Our kiss intensified, and Anthony pulled my leg up over his hip, grinding into me. Slowly, sensual … delicious. I wound my fingers into his hair and tugged him closer, whimpering at the passion growing larger and larger inside of me. The television was the only noise in the background as we fit together perfectly, rocking, and whimpering ourselves to orgasm, holding onto each other as if we would never be able to let go.

CHRISTMAS

Being a mother is learning about strengths you didn't know you had and dealing with fears you didn't know existed.

Linda Wooten

Self-discovery is a journey of leaving a mundane life of existing and believing that there is something more. Self-discovery is not about discovering who you are but uncovering who you are. It's uncomfortable and can hurt, but it's in that discomfort that we grow and become the person we were meant to be. Sometimes it comes during an adventure—a trip with friends perhaps. Sometimes it comes with a new career or new role. And sometimes … with a love so passionate, so explosive, you almost can't trust this new person you uncover as your "true" self.

At times through my marriage I have loved enough for the both of us. I loved Anthony enough to put my own life on hold so I could raise our children and be Mrs. Anthony Bello. The perfect wife and mother who kept a beautiful home, always had meals on the table, volunteering at my children's school, and running a few very successful fundraisers. I gave love with no strings attached.

If I had to be true to myself, it's only through my children that I know what pure love is … I know I'm a good mother. To survive and grow, I have to accept that I'm a being made up of conflicted contradictions. I'm practical and I'm also unrealistic. I'm loyal and I'm willing to risk that loyalty at the same time. I'm intelligent and also inclined to be naive. And, I also have to accept that my marriage has become a never-ending paradox.

Julia

★ ★ ★

A week went by with no word from Sebastian. Usually he was the talker; in the past I had been the one to ignore messages. It was strange that now he was the one being distant from me. Was it truly over? It was almost too much to bear. The only way I was holding myself together was by staying busy. We were hosting Anthony's work Christmas party, plus I wanted the house to be extra perfect this year for Matteo and Adriana's wedding.

Christmas was a time of year when I went all out—trying to combine exuberant festivities with a sophisticated styling. I always had a bit of anxiety when we got closer to Christmas. It was my own fault because I wanted everyone to be happy; the memories of my children running around our home when they were younger made me long for those days of believing in Santa and drawing pictures of reindeer.

Our children, so precious and wonderful. They had grown up so quickly. Sometimes it was difficult to connect my memories of them with the people they had become. Mia begging to put the star on top of the tree; Camilla spending ages decorating her cookies, her tongue sticking out in concentration long after the others had decided to run off and play; Matteo helping his younger sisters unwrap their gifts.

It was all about family, and this year Adriana would officially be a member of the Bello clan. The wedding was going to be beautiful, but so difficult at the same time. Gaining a daughter, but in some way losing my son—my child. And my mom and Anthony's mom wouldn't be there. My mother would so have loved to see her grandchild get married. I could envision her here, sitting at our dining room table, tipsy on one glass of wine and giving Adriana recipes for Christmas dishes. She would be telling stories to amuse the kids and eating an extra helping of tiramisu.

She always had so much advice. She would be telling Matteo the same things she had told me. My mother was my rock; whenever I needed advice or a hug, she was there. I missed her so, so much. I wondered what advice she would give me now, in light of the direction that my life had taken. My mother would have been disappointed in my choices. She had always told me things as they were. Firm but caring. I needed her guidance.

To be forever happy, that seemed almost unattainable, as did most things in my life right now. It was strange to me that the two men I so desperately loved I couldn't fully have. Sebastian was as connected to me as I had ever felt to another human being. We were perfectly matched; we mirrored each other. And yet he wasn't here with me. Anthony … Anthony was with me, but not connected. They each offered one half of what I needed. I felt lost and confused.

I LOVE YOU STILL

In times like these I wished I could talk to my mom. She had steadied me on my wedding day, and soon enough I would be doing the same for my daughters. I could almost hear her imparting that sage wisdom that truly would carry me not only through that day, but in some ways the rest of my married life—at least up until now.

"Tesoro," my mom sang as she waltzed back into the room. "Look at you!"

I smiled nervously, taking another sip of champagne, trying to ease the butterflies.

"Vanessa did a great job on your hair," she said. I agreed. My hair and makeup were styled to look natural; Anthony loved my natural beauty, and I was dressing for him. I wanted him to see me as the woman he would spend the rest of his life with, the woman he had fallen in love with.

"Julia Teresa," my mother said. "Sei bellissima, Il trucco è bello, cara, ma la bellezza viene da te. Il tuo amore è ciò che ti fa brillare. La bellezza di una sposa viene sempre da dentro. Quando sei felice si vede. Se brilli dentro, brilli anche al di fuori."

(Makeup is lovely, dear, but the beauty comes from you. Your love is what makes you glow. A bride's beauty always comes from within. When you're happy, it shows. If you sparkle from the inside, you sparkle on the outside too.)

I felt tears spring to my eyes.

"Thanks, mama. I really love Anthony so much. And I can't wait to be his wife."

She cupped my cheeks in her hands.

"I know, bella. And it's perfectly normal to feel a little nervous. This is the most serious commitment you will ever make in your life, and yet it's such a joyous one. We're all with you, to celebrate such a blessed event."

I gulped.

"That's what's making me nervous. Anthony I'm certain about. But what if I mess up? There are so many people here."

"So many people who love you," she reminded me. "Cara, on my wedding day, I was certain that I was going to fall flat on my face, put your father's ring on the wrong finger, but do you know what happened? The moment I saw him, I stopped worrying. When you see the man you love waiting at the end of the aisle to make you his forever … it's the most amazing feeling in the world. And if you do fall or step on his feet while dancing … we can just give everyone more alcohol, and they won't remember a thing."

I choked on laughter, pulling my mom into a tight hug.

"I love you," I told her.

"I love you too, cara. Now, shall we put on that fabulous tiara?"

I had decided to wear my mother's tiara. It was so elegant and sparkly, and hers. I loved it. With my long veil and elaborate dress line, I felt like a fairytale princess, off to marry my prince.

I hoped Adriana would experience the same thing. Every girl deserves to feel like the luckiest person in the world on their wedding day. I was sure she would be a beautiful bride. She and Matteo were as in love as any two people could be. I prayed that they would be happy together for the rest of their lives, that they wouldn't grow apart as the years went by, but instead grow as one.

Snow was swirling gently outside. The trees were coated, and the windowsill was rapidly becoming carpeted. The house was warm and golden from the lights I had just hung; nothing felt more peaceful and merrier than Christmas. I pulled some handmade ornaments out of the box made by my children. Every year I asked them to make a new one. The last few years Matt hadn't, but his sisters still had. It was only a matter of time until they refused too. They would become busy with their own lives.

I held a felt elf hat that Mia had made in primary school in one hand, and a snow globe that Camilla had made in craft club in the other. Matteo's wooden Santa was on the table in front of me. I liked to have one ornament from each of them in front of the tree.

Anthony came up behind me and picked out a "sleigh" that Camilla had drawn and laminated when she was four or five.

"I think it's time to retire this one to the back of the tree," he joked. As always, I knew he wouldn't. He placed it in clear view every year. It was something precious that our daughter had made; why couldn't he just say out loud how much he cherished it?

He had always been a very proper man in front of others, saving his true emotions and vulnerability for me, and me alone. Then he had shared some of it with our children. His vows to me had been so very beautiful; I remembered them word for word.

My beautiful Julia, I say these vows to you today not just as promises I make, but as privileges I will honor. To live a life with you as husband and wife, to laugh and cry with you, care for you, raise a family with you. Most amazing is that I get to love you forever, till death do us part. You're my now and you're my future. Without you, I can't see what tomorrow or the next day, or the one after that look like. You make the picture complete. You make me complete.

THE BELLO WEDDING

Tell me who admires and loves you, and I will tell you who you are.

Charles Augustin Sainte-Beuve

My Dearest Son,

My heart is full as I sit to write this letter to you on the morning of your wedding day. I pray you receive it with all the love I have in my heart. Son, life is full of swift transitions and time passes so fast. Twenty-five years ago, you came into my life. I will never forget that day. You were such a beautiful baby, with a hint of reddish gold hair, angelic face, beautiful brown eyes. As I held you in my arms, I wondered what the future held for you, for us. I prayed to God to help me be a good mother and to protect and guide you the best that I could. Matteo, today as you wed your beloved, I can only wish for you the same good things that I wanted with your father. I wish you patience, so that you can accept that no one is perfect. I wish you strength, so that you can always put Adrianna's well-being first. And I wish that you both learn to accept the bad qualities and love the good qualities without guilt and without expectations of perfection. My son, always share your true self with Adriana, flaws and all; vulnerability reveals our greatest strength and also our greatest weakness. Weather the storm together and never let go of the feeling you have today as you wed your bride.

With Love Always,
Mom

★ ★ ★

Adriana looked absolutely stunning; I couldn't stop the tears as she glided down the aisle. Her hair was styled in a simple loose braid with a couple of small peonies tucked in one side. The splash of pink against the ivory gown was lovely, her cheeks excitedly blushed. The way she looked at Matteo, it seemed as if he was the only person there. It was visible to everyone how badly she just wanted to run and jump into his arms. Matteo's jaw dropped when he first saw her, as if he couldn't believe his luck.

It wasn't only for this day; they had both existed in a world only of each other since they had met. Neither of them seemed to ever waver in their affections, and I prayed that they would stay this way forever. So happy and full of hope. They were taking this step together, building their own life and family.

I sniffed into my hankie, trying not to ruin my makeup. While the ceremony was small and intimate, I knew that there would be numerous photos taken. It wouldn't do for the mother of the groom to be sobbing in all of them.

Adriana reached the flowered arch and took Matteo's hands with a happy squeal that made her husband-to-be laugh, eliciting a few giggles from their family and friends as well. Anthony chuckled next to me and put an arm around my shoulders. Our son, our little boy, all grown up and marrying this lovely girl. So happy and genuine. She was honestly all that we could have hoped for.

Matteo's vows only managed to make me cry harder, Anthony squeezing my hand tightly as I sobbed.

"Adriana. You're the most beautiful woman in the world. From the first moment I saw you, I knew that you would be special to me. While our interests may be different, our souls are the same. I promise to be true to you, love and protect you forever, and even go to the spa with you as many times as you wish. I would even get my toenails painted for you, so long as you remain the moon of my life."

Several of the guests laughed, and I frowned at Anthony.

"*Game of Thrones* reference," he whispered.

"Ah," I nodded. That made sense. He was recognizing her wants while also showing his own interests. The way she smiled back at him was gorgeous.

"As you wish," she teased, interrupting his vows, "my sun and stars."

At that, Matt did a little fist pump and his friends cheered. He then turned back to his bride and kissed her on the cheek.

I assumed that was also a *Game of Thrones* reference. I decided then and there that Anthony and I really must watch it together. Matteo then continued his declarations to the woman that he would spend the rest of his life with.

"Dri, no one else in the world will ever be able to hold a candle to you. I love the way you bring me coffee in bed when I'm ignoring my alarm clock, and the way you sob through romantic movies. I even adore your humming as you get ready in the morning, and that you always leave the cap off the toothpaste. You drive me crazy, and being able to now call you my wife, Mrs. Adriana Bello, makes me feel like the luckiest man in the world."

Adriana's father teared up. I tried sending him a comforting smile, but he didn't look my way. I understood exactly how he felt. At that moment, we were all so perfectly attuned while watching our children take their next step in life.

Adriana sniffed delicately, and Matteo gently wiped away a couple of stray tears from the corners of her eyes.

"Matteo," she began, her voice cracking slightly, "I love you more than I ever thought that I could love anyone. You have brought me so much joy, and yet we're only at the start of our journey. Your dedication and loving nature will make you a wonderful husband, your patience and presence will make you a wonderful father, and your enthusiasm for trying new things, for expanding our horizons, will make you the best friend that I could ever have. I look forward to growing with you. I see your *Game of Thrones*, my sun and stars, and I raise you a *Star Wars*: Will you be the Han to my Leila?"

Again, a small chuckle of laughter rippled through the audience, with one of Matteo's friends loudly whistling and cheering. *Perfect,* I thought. *They are perfect for each other.*

Their joy was apparent in the tight hug they shared before their sweet kiss. A peck on the lips, but so loving, it made my heart melt. I could hear my sisters awing behind me and turned to see them give a thumbs-up. As my son and new daughter-in-law sat themselves to sign the register, I struggled to stay seated. I had the urge to go up and hug them.

Anthony kissed my head as he stood. The happy couple had decided to have their fathers as their witnesses—it had begun as a joke, as the two young lawyers laughed that Adriana's father, a district attorney, would definitely make the marriage official. Having Anthony step up then only felt right; two fathers, bonding together their children. The beautiful ceremony concluded, the guests, some still teary-eyed, headed off to the reception.

After an incredibly sweet first dance with his bride, Matteo came up to me and held out his hand.

"Give me the pleasure of this dance, dearest mother?"

I grinned and stood, mimicking a curtsy. "As you wish, good sir."

We fell easily into the slow dance; I felt so proud of my boy. So handsome, so grown up.

"Do you remember teaching me to dance?" he asked. "When I was small, and I wanted to dance with Zia?"

"Yes," I laughed. "You were an outrageous flirt for a seven-year-old. You wouldn't dance with the other children at all—you only wanted to dance with the grown-up ladies. You only got away with it because you were so damn cute."

"Well it paid off, didn't it? If anyone is videoing this, we look pretty good if I do say so myself."

"We do indeed." We turned in a circle, following the rhythm of the music.

"I'm so, so proud of you," I told him. "You have grown into such a wonderful man."

"Thanks, Mom." His eyes crinkled as he grinned, looking so much like his father. "You and Dad clearly did a good job."

I playfully swatted him. "Cheeky!"

He pulled me back into our dance posture and continued stepping in time.

"Seriously, you and Dad raised us so well Mom. I don't think I'd be where I am today without your support. If I haven't said it today, thank you Mom. I love you."

"I love you too. Your father and I always believed in you," I assured him. "I know you would never let something so wonderful slip through your fingers."

He shook his head. "It's not just being married to Adriana. It's also about being a husband she will be proud of. You and Dad gave us a pretty good example to follow. You taught us the value of hard work, family, and love. You did good Mom. Thank you."

I felt myself tear up again. My makeup surely was completely ruined by this point, but I had stopped caring. What would a wedding be without some maternal tears shed?

"We tried, Matteo. I'm so glad you feel that way. All we wanted was to give you and your sisters a happy home and good moments in life to remember." We stopped dancing, and Matteo kissed my cheek.

"Well you both succeeded. Thank you for my letter, it may or may not have made me tear up. I love you Mom."

"I love you too, darling."

I sniffled and choked out a laugh as Matt sauntered over to his numerous "aunties," my sisters. Some biological and some not, all of them playfully rolled their eyes as he approached them. Eventually Filomena gave in and allowed him to charm her onto the makeshift dance floor.

As the wedding was inside an old restored barn at their favorite winery, Matteo and Adriana had made a few compromises for the sake of convenience. Strong wooden pallets were nailed together and painted white to form a contiguous dancing surface. They both loved the outdoors and wanted to celebrate their wedding, even in winter. The barn was agreed on by all as it brought the outdoors inside, especially with the large picture windows—it had started snowing heavily and felt so magical.

I ambled slowly back to the table where Anthony sat with our two daughters, trying to engage them in a game of chess. The gathering would last well into the night; the newlyweds had wanted a fun, relaxed environment. Each table had a board game on it, modified slightly to represent the happy couple. The chess set had the king and queen switched out to a bride and groom.

A trio of Matteo's friends were cheering as someone won a match, their table littered with empty beer bottles and cards. Adriana was playing with Sophia's daughters further away. She had set up a giant Jenga set with them in mind, and it was lovely to see her laughing and hugging them. It was a shame she was an only child; I could just see a young Adriana doting on her little brothers or sisters. It made me smile to think of her as a mother one day.

One of her girlfriends joined them, chucking a large soft ball into the mix, and gently tackling my tiny niece into the ground, loud chimes of laughter ensuing. It made me miss the time when Mia and Camilla were that age.

I seated myself beside my family and nodded toward the little ones.

"I remember when you were that small," I told them.

"Mom," Mia frowned. "Do you have to?"

"Reminisce about my children? Absolutely. You all used to be so small. You guys used to worship us," I teased.

Anthony nodded. "It's true. You thought we were the most amazing people in the world. And you thought we were cool."

"And how many people did we know at that point, Dad?" Camilla giggled.

"Loads," he insisted. "We had friends come over all the time."

Father and daughter looked as if they were willing to debate it; Fran skipped over bearing two glasses of prosecco.

"Want to have a little wander?" she asked. "I see a rather snowy tree that we can stand under and take a selfie. Probably get completely soaked, but I want that picture."

I laughed. "I'll go for a walk, but I'm not going to risk any snow falling on this expensive dress."

Fran snorted, rather unladylike. "If Adriana isn't bothered, then I don't think the rest of us should be."

It was true; the hem of Adriana's gown was getting damp as she ran outside with the children, eager to catch snowflakes on their tongues. The pale grey of her fur shrug kept her warm and looked wonderful with the sweetheart neckline and delicate beading of her dress. The draping of the skirt made an elegant silhouette; it was really sweet how the little ones all called her Princess Adriana.

"This wedding is absolutely gorgeous," Fran commented. "It suits them so well."

"It really does," I replied. "It's so lovely to see them have the wedding that they really want."

"It's certainly a freer generation. Do you remember the weddings we all had?"

"Yes!" I exclaimed. "Do you remember how large Sophia's skirt was?"

"She could barely get through the door."

"Like you're one to talk," we heard Alex say, as we turned to see her joining us. "With your poufy shoulders!"

I laughed. "You had a massive bow on the back of your dress," I retorted.

Fran chuckled and took a sip of her bubbly.

"Hey!" Alex and I cried indignantly.

"We remember the length of your train," I pointed out to my laughing friend.

"Hopefully, you will wear something more practical next time," Alex added with a wink. "You know, when Alessandro sweeps you off your feet and pops the question."

Francesca blushed and swatted at Alexandra. "You assume too much my good lady. I'm fine with living in sin."

The banter continued long into the night, the alcohol warming us enough to not notice the weather getting colder as the moon and stars came out. The children were all asleep, but the adults looked on with youthful glee as fireworks were set off. Adriana's eyes shone as she watched them, and Matteo's eyes shone as he watched her.

THE WHOLE TRUTH

*A woman has to live her life, or live to repent
not having lived it.*

D. H. Lawrence

Slowly we end what we started. I sometimes wonder whether what you felt was real. Did you mean all of those sentiments you whispered in my ear? Did you make me fall in love with you through lies? Deception or desperation, maybe a bit of both?

It's so ironic that you were the one to convince me to live in two worlds. You told me how lucky I was to have found two loves in a single lifetime when there are people who never even find one. You asked me to live a secret life with you. You promised to be my refuge in my time of need, to give me a break from my reality when I needed it. Two worlds, one woman, two men, one love, split in two to make me whole.

Yes, you convinced me that I deserved this kind of love. I believed you and I completely let you in and now you have let me down. You left me just when I needed you most. And, even though you broke my heart. I will never regret loving you, because for me it was real, even if it was for a short time.

You will always be a chapter in my story. After all, love stories couldn't end if they didn't begin.

Julia

★ ★ ★

Anthony was more attentive to me in the week following the wedding. He made me coffee in the morning before he went to work and came home on time on the days that he said he would. I knew it wouldn't last, and yet some part of me still hoped it would. He was trying, and I couldn't sabotage it by being skeptical.

However, this new wave of happiness didn't explain my continued need to message Sebastian. He had been out of my life for months now. I shared a photo of Matteo and Adriana, laughing as they leaned in for a kiss. While my husband was rarely if ever mentioned, Sebastian and I had always loved talking about our children. I knew that he would be so happy for me. I waited anxiously for a response as I flicked through the rest of the photos on my laptop, looking for the ones I would like to frame.

I found the one—Adriana sliding Matteo's ring onto his finger. It was a beautiful, non-staged shot of the couple. I considered framing others as well. I had photos from each phase of my children's lives. Of course, I didn't want to take up too much space with pictures of Matteo and Adriana, yet it was truly the event I was most proud of to date.

Sebastian's lack of reply was worrying me. Had I crossed a line somehow?

It was two days later that I finally heard from him. Unfortunately, I heard from someone else first. I was so on edge, hoping for Sebastian's reply, so I hadn't checked the number when my phone rang. I picked up to only a slight crackling on the other end of the line.

"Hello." There was no response. This sounded very much like a telemarketer, and I sighed as I hung up. Moments later, it rang again. I picked up, ready to give whomever it was a piece of my mind. But this time I heard a woman's voice respond, a voice that was soft but confident, with a steely edge.

"Who are you?" I asked.

"My name is Daniela DeLuca," she announced, "and I'm asking you to stay away from my son … or else."

My skin prickled. Who the hell did the woman think she was? I knew little of her from Sebastian. She had been neglectful during his childhood, and they had a poor relationship now. This was most definitely overstepping a line. I was certain that Sebastian was unaware of her phoning me.

"Does Sebastian know that you're calling me?"

"He doesn't need to," she snapped. "I'm his mother."

I took a deep breath. "I know who you are Mrs. DeLuca. I have no hold on your son. He's a grown man, capable of making his own choices. Now, are you threatening me?"

"Mrs. Bello … I'm telling you to stay away and focus on your husband. If you don't, then you and your family will suffer the consequences."

"How dare you! What do you mean my family?" I shrieked, but Daniela had already hung up. I was shaking with anger; I needed clarification. What *did* she mean? I couldn't bear my family suffering because of my involvement with Sebastian. She was in Italy. Would she really come here and reveal all to Anthony, or was she bluffing? She could certainly afford to.

I couldn't wrap my head around Mrs. DeLuca's intentions. I needed to speak to Sebastian. He was the only one who could fix this. My hands shook as I dialed his number, praying that he would pick up. Each ring was agony, my stomach churning with fear. Fight or flight? I knew I needed to fight.

"Julia," he said, his tone full of happiness. He didn't know. "How are you, my love? This is a surprise."

"Sebastian," I managed, my voice riddled with tears. "Your mother, she just called me, and she … she … threatened me. Oh my god! She told me there would be consequences. My family, she threatened them too. She … she … said…"

I couldn't finish my sentence. It was too awful. Besides, would he even believe me? This was his mother after all. Regardless of distance, they were connected by blood. To us, with our large Italian families, blood was sacred. You didn't betray blood, no matter the circumstances.

The pause was deafening, punctuated only by my sobbing. I was certain that Sebastian would put me down or hang up. He did neither.

"Calm down. It's okay. I promise I'll take care of it," he said firmly. "You don't need to worry about Daniela. I'll make sure that she stays away from you and your family. You're precious to me; as precious as any family, amore. She has no place in my life or yours. I won't let her terrorize you. Don't worry. Please just stop crying."

His words calmed me. She would stay away from me. And Sebastian viewed me as family. The doubt and fear lingered, but now it was at least somewhat under control. I had to trust him. After all, how could there be any immediate threat when Sebastian had just given me his word that he would protect me? I would be okay. We would be okay.

Regardless, I couldn't shake the feeling that something was terribly wrong. Why would Daniela DeLuca threaten me? And why would Sebastian just dismiss it so easily rather than discussing it with me fully? His descriptions of her in the past had been vague at best.

I opened up my laptop and started searching for answers. I had never seen a Facebook entry for Sebastian, but then again to do so would be to mix my two lives together. In a way, it would be flaunting my affair with Sebastian right in front of Anthony. I clicked the search bar and typed before I changed my mind.

```
Sebastian DeLuca
```

What seemed like hundreds of results came up; I scrolled through with purpose. Too young, too old, too fat, too bald ... none of them were "my" Sebastian. I sighed. With no mutual friends and living so far apart, it was like searching for a needle in a haystack. I searched again.

```
Daniela DeLuca
```

It was much the same as my search for Sebastian, but it did give me some much-needed inspiration.

```
Luciano DeLuca
```

Finally, results. There wouldn't be a profile, of course; Sebastian's father had been dead for years. But a couple of old translated newspaper articles and comments surfaced.

I LOVE YOU STILL

I clenched my jaw as I prepared to enter my lover's world. Was this betraying his trust? Would he be angry if he knew more? It felt wrong in some way. I should just tell him about how scared I really was about Daniela. I should just ask him to explain it to me further.

I couldn't stop myself. I clicked on the first article, evidently scanned from an Italian newspaper copy. I immediately wished I hadn't; there were two large photos surrounded by a small print. The first, of Marcello, only briefly caught my attention. It was the second that caught me off guard. Luciano DeLuca, with wife Daniela and son Sebastian. The boy in the picture looked so happy, clinging to his smiling parents. It almost hurt to look at, understanding that family would come to be torn apart.

Mob Boss Murdered in Family Restaurant

Father and son found dead yesterday while dining, three hours apart - Martino Meucci for the Positano Quotidiano.

Two men have been publicly murdered as of yesterday, April 17. Marcello and Luciano DeLuca were killed 500km and three hours apart, both while dining in public.

Emergency responders were called to Florence at 6:30 p.m. after Marcello DeLuca was shot during a business meeting at the Terracotta Ristorante on Monday. The bullet passed through his throat, and Mr. DeLuca, 58, was declared dead at the scene five minutes later. Similarly, his son Luciano, aged 39, was having a quiet dinner with friends in Positano, at the Cabernet Ristorante, when he was gunned down at 9:30 p.m. Both men were shot by snipers positioned across the street from the restaurant and hit through the glass of the building. Both apartments were vacant when police entered, and neighbors were unable to identify any unusual behavior prior to the attacks. Both men were purportedly in good health prior to the incident. There have been no reports of antisocial behavior at either restaurant on the evening in question.

The DeLucas are well known throughout Italy for their underground activities in numerous illegal ventures. DeLuca senior was previously charged with theft and arson in 1952 and released on bail, followed by a prison sentence in '56 for possession of class A substances. Since then, the DeLucas have toed the line between their business interests and law enforcement. On April 17, it is reported that Marcello DeLuca was meeting with the head of the Mafioso family, and several successful developers, in a purely diplomatic role to negotiate property sales on their behalf. Further investigation into these claims are currently under way.

I LOVE YOU STILL

Savera Pivirotto, who is a 28-year-old fashion designer, was enjoying a meal with her husband and two daughters when the hit took place on the DeLuca family patriarch. "It was horrific," she said. "I don't remember ever seeing so much blood. I was terrified for my family; my children were utterly inconsolable. They are afraid to be apart from us. It's just shocking that something like this could happen in such a popular establishment. We've been going there for years." Similarly, Marco Correale was having an early supper with his elderly parents at the time. "We were just settling the bill when it happened. It was shocking, just shocking. My mum started sobbing, and dad just didn't know what to do. I just had to get them out of there as quickly as possible. The police didn't want anyone to leave the scene, but I had to insist on giving my statement first. My mum is 79, for Christ's sake!"

Luciano DeLucas wife, Daniela [pictured above] has refused to comment. A family friend has asked that the DeLucas be left alone during this difficult time.

Two men have been detained regarding these events. Chief of Police, Antonio Rodia, has asked that if anyone has any information, to please contact law enforcement ASAP.

It was worse than I had imagined. One of the most prominent crime families, now apparently headed by Sebastian's mother. I was amazed that Sebastian had become the man he was, surrounded nearly all his life by violence and fear, and yet he had grown to be a polite, hardworking gentleman with a love of poetry. Why hadn't he told me the truth?

He was so caring, and so protective of his daughter. Probably a response to his own upbringing. He needed love and support following the deaths of his father and grandfather, on the same day no less, and instead his mother had withdrawn from him, leaving him with his uncle, and sending him off to France. What kind of cold-hearted woman was she? Who was I dealing with and what was she really capable of?

Reading the article made my heart bleed, and I knew that I hadn't heard the last from Daniela DeLuca.

January 1

Why would I phone Sebastian of all people? I know that I need to move on. And at New Year's no less? I just couldn't resist the chance to ring in the New Year with a man that I loved; I called via video chat. The fireworks around me didn't make up for the lack of fireworks that I felt inside. How can I ever be happy knowing that I've lost something so unknown to me? And then, for me to see the woman with him. Blonde, tall, buxom, disheveled. Younger than me, and in many ways she appeared my opposite. How had he been attracted to me at all if she was his type? Just a friend he says. He assured me he didn't sleep with her while we were together, but I don't think I can ever know for sure.

I LOVE YOU STILL

My heart sank as the fireworks exploded overhead. My drunk husband reached for me, pressing a kiss to my lips; for me though, the world was a haze—almost as if it was spinning in slow motion. There were so many people, so many friends at our home, and yet none truly understood me. Most of them were Anthony's friends; my friends had left earlier to tend to their families. The only people remaining were those whose children were otherwise entertained on the busiest night of the year, and those that were Anthony's drinking buddies.

My priorities weren't aligned with those of the exuberant partiers. I was grateful, as always, for the New Year. I prayed and thanked the Lord for the fortune bestowed on my family in the last year. The wonderful moments that we had shared together and the difficulties that we had overcome. I smiled up at the heavens, knowing that my son was happily at home with his new wife, quietly ringing in the New Year with the woman that he chose to be with for the rest of his life. And my girls were celebrating together, skiing in Quebec.

None of this changed the absence of something missing inside of me. What I felt was more of a tempered joy, muted by the emptiness in my heart. The missing puzzle piece for me was of course Sebastian. The wine that I had steadily sipped throughout the evening coursed through me, and I felt weighted down as I retired into the quiet of my living room, unnoticed by my now relatively drunken husband. If I phoned Sebastian, would he answer? What would he be doing? I wondered whether he would be spending the occasion with her. I wondered whether I should risk it.

Before I knew what I was doing my phone was in my hand and I was attempting to video call Sebastian. *Please, please, Sebastian. Please pick up.*

The phone continued to ring, and my eyes welled up. Unavailable. Maybe he hadn't heard it ring? The wine urged me to try one more time.

"Please," I whispered desperately. "Please. I need you."

I sank back into the couch cushions behind me, folding my legs up to press my knees against my chest. I could still hear the loud shouts and chuckles of laughter from outside, but I felt oddly safe in my sanctuary. The closed door to the empty room offered me relief—a place to be as I was, rather than what I was expected to be. My children absent, my husband entertaining our guests, I was surrounded by people, and still I was welcoming the new year alone.

Finally, the call connected, and my heart rose in my chest. He had answered! I just wanted him to share the moment with me. His face was as handsome as ever, lit up with joy. Was he so happy to hear from me? The thought buoyed me.

"Julia!" He sang my name.

"Sebastian, how are you? I'm sorry for calling so late," I babbled. "I just wanted to wish you a Happy New Year. I didn't know whether you would be busy or anything, but …"

"Julia," he laughed, "slow down. Happy New Year, amore mio."

"Sorry," I sighed. "I should have messaged first, but it looks like you're at home at least …"

"Well, my love, it *is* early morning here."

"Oh!" I gasped. "I'm sorry, did I wake you?"

"Not at all," he reassured me. "We haven't slept yet, so you have picked a good time."

We? Did he have someone with him? I couldn't see or hear anyone there …

"I hope I'm not interrupting anything," I murmured numbly. "I shouldn't have called …"

"You can always call me, Julia," he assured me.

"Just hearing your voice, knowing that you're okay, it …" I didn't finish my sentence after I heard a woman call his name.

"Sebastian," a high-pitched, definitely female voice called out; his head whipped around fast to smile at the woman off camera. My heart stopped. There was someone there … a woman. "Who are you talking to?"

I cleared my throat awkwardly as she came into view. She was so young. Mid to late twenties if I had to guess. She was curvaceous, tousled blonde hair that rested against generous cleavage. Even on my small phone screen, I could see that she wasn't wearing a bra. Her perky nipples stood proudly, visible through the thin layer of skintight fabric that stretched around her silhouette. A short-sleeved cropped T-shirt and jeans, and yet even dressed casually she looked stunning. I bit back the tears that threatened my loss of dignity.

He had said that he would always love me. Even now, he told me that he still wanted to hear my voice. He still called me his amore. And yet he did so while another woman was with him, looking freshly fucked. My heart, though, told me that he had never lied to me. Every word, every kiss, every shared poem told a different story. Still, was I so desperate for love that I was so readily convinced of a bond that never existed?

"Julia," he interrupted my thoughts, still smiling. "This is Morgan, a friend of mine. Morgan, Julia."

"Hi, Julia!" Morgan sang. "It's so lovely to finally meet you—Sebastian has told me so much about you. You're exactly as he described."

And how had he described me? Why would he tell some stranger about me?

"Ahh, hi, Morgan," I replied, a wooden smile on my lips. "Happy New Year. Anyway, I was just phoning to say that, so I'll let you two get on with your day. Goodnight, or rather good morning," I giggled, the sound forced and frightening. "Bye."

I hung up before either had a chance to reply. I turned off the phone. What the fuck just happened? I wouldn't be tempted to call again. Never again.

SOFT SISTERS IN IRELAND

As you share your hearts with one another. May they always be loyal and true. And friendship be between you in all that you do.

Irish proverb

I believe that women should inspire one another. Meaningful, lasting friendships are one-of-a-kind treasures. You don't go looking for these friends; they are part of your fate, and you were destined to meet them somewhere along the way. Some may stay and some may go, but all teach you something about yourself. Then of course, there are those special few—your soul sisters.

I prefer to preserve my energy for those special few. They stand with you through the challenges. Regardless of how long you may be apart or how far the distance, you know that you can count on them—just as I have always counted on my "sisters." These friendships have proven unbreakable, and for that I'm so very grateful. We have created our own world, and perhaps not everyone can understand that world, or the nature of our bond, but it doesn't matter. We are a family, a sisterhood. We even came up with our own name of SOFT, "Sisters of Fabulous Times"—this is who we are. We don't give up on each other. In fact, we will protect each other and have each other's backs for life.

Julia

★ ★ ★

I managed to push aside my worries about the DeLuca family over the next few months, focusing on my family and planning the summer trip with my sisters and friends. I occasionally heard from Sebastian, but our messages were short, and our topics remained in safe categories. Nothing too intense, both of us shying away from the things that we really wanted to talk about but couldn't. I was proud of the fact that I hadn't called him or wanted to see him after that embarrassing night.

Before I knew it, I was away with the girls, leaving my everyday life behind. Our trip to Ireland passed far too quickly, the whole country being new to us, and the fun and vibrancy of Dublin providing a much faster pace than that of Italy. While Italy is famed for wine, Dublin is the home of Guinness. What kind of tourists would we be if we didn't indulge?

The plan was to fill our days in the Emerald Isle with castles and bookstores, our nights with pubs, and of course the aforementioned Guinness. A country known for rolling green hills, a lush countryside with breathtaking views regardless of which direction you look, not to mention a bevy of cute men to boot—which made Fran and Filomena happy—Ireland ultimately proved to be everything we had hoped it would be.

We decided to spend our first night in the seaside town of Cobh—this, the historic last port for the Titanic before it's fateful disaster. We actually booked into the museum for a tour. A virtual experience of a ship that most thought unsinkable; here you are given a boarding pass for one of the one hundred and twenty-three passengers who boarded the ill-fated liner in 1912. At the end of the tour you have the unique and very somber experience of finding out who "your passenger" was, why they were boarding the Titanic, and whether they survived. In some ways, it was difficult to comprehend the horror of what they must have felt. Afterward we sat and talked through the night about the emotions that we had felt, and we shared the stories of the passengers we had experienced.

The next morning, I took off on my own for a bit. I just wanted to clear my head, take in the beauty of the scenery before me and write. Writing on this particular trip would become my escape in some ways, my go-to when I needed to make heads or tails of what I was feeling, and of what I really wanted out of life. I met a young man at the local coffee shop; his name was Kieran, and we struck up a conversation. He was certainly an energetic one and seemed to become excited while relating to me the story of the spirits of Cobh. He told me he believed that the town was also known for witchcraft; the people of the village were well acquainted with both the good and the bad spirits that never leave the scenic Victorian locale.

Later that day, I recounted all of this to Alexandra. She, like me, was somewhat frazzled by the tale. We decided not only to lock but barricade our bedroom doors with our luggage.

Cobh itself might be described as quaint, but after hearing the stories of ghosts, we believed it to be on the sketchier side—at least the section our Airbnb was in. Filomena, not taking any chances that spirit or person alike would overcome her, opted to sleep with a pair of scissors and a barricaded door as well that night. It was definitely an experience we weren't expecting.

The next morning, we discovered Irish soda bread with butter. Soft, rich, decadent … it was the perfect way to kick off the day, oh so satisfying. I don't think I had ever tasted anything quite like it. Then again, the moonshine with which we filled out newly purchased flasks wasn't that bad either. What can I say? We were on vacation after all.

We had planned a bus tour to visit the Cliffs of Moher—a decidedly different experience than at Cobh. This was about exhilaration, feeling on top of the world in some ways, laughing and singing. In fact, Francesca and I were racing to the bus; last one there had to sing. I won. Francesca thus belted out the Pointer Sisters' 'I'm So Excited.' Definitely appropriate for the occasion. She sang as only she could. She loved the attention and got a standing ovation incidentally.

Sophia and I held onto each other for dear life as we attempted the climb to the top. The winds were crazy. So crazy in fact, that an old man was ceremoniously toppled, and the paramedics had to be called. We continued on after we made sure he was okay. Standing at the top of the Cliffs of Moher, looking out over the cool grays and icy blues of the Atlantic Ocean, was in some ways fulfilling a long-held dream of mine. This was heaven—it had to be. I thought of my mom; places like this reminded me of her. My bird's-eye view removed from the otherwise craziness and tumult of life for a moment.

We somehow got separated from Filomena, Alexandra, and Francesca. Given the lack of cell service, we had no way to get a hold of them. So, my sister Sophia and I ended up just enjoying the experience together. It also gave me alone time with my little sister. We were able to talk a bit about life. I told her how proud I was of her and that she was doing a great job in raising her girls. I know she needed to hear it.

Upon returning to the tour bus, there was still no sign of the others. The bus driver couldn't have been less impressed. We begged him to wait just five more minutes. After twenty minutes had passed, he had had enough and was leaving, come hell or high water. Thankfully, we spotted them running behind the bus, screaming, "Stop! Stop!" with their arms flailing. The driver relented and eventually stopped, informing the tardy trio to count their Irish blessings that he had waited for them after all. We drank the flasks of moonshine on the drive home and laughed at the trouble we seemed to always cause.

Our very last day in Ireland was spent exploring Dublin. And the famous Temple Bar was definitely one of the highlights—for a few reasons—namely, Colin, Seamus, Patrick, Liam, Cillian, and Aiden. They were gentlemen, and what's more, they were terrifically fun to be around, and how refreshing it was that they happened to be our age.

Aiden and I hit it off quite well, platonically speaking of course. I wasn't going to give any man more than conversation, that's it; I certainly didn't need more male attention, trust me, not given my current situation. So, it was very nice to have an engaging conversation with a man with no strings attached. He made me laugh, purely so without the worry of what my husband or lover were thinking in the back of their minds. It was wonderful actually.

Seamus was flirting with Fran, and of course she was lapping it up as only Fran could.

"Have you ever kissed an Irishman before?" he teased, to which Fran answered, "No, I haven't." Seamus then predictably and still somewhat charmingly responded, "Would you like to kiss an Irishman lass?"

"Damn, I wish I could, but I'm kissing Italian right now. God, you're cute! I love Irish men." Fran has always been a quick wit. The interaction, I could see, had made her a bit giddy, almost reverting to a jubilant girlishness. They hit it off and consequently flirted all night. I wondered briefly about Alessandro. Where did he factor into the scene playing out in the Temple Bar? Was she having second thoughts perhaps? But I tried to put it out of my mind. This wasn't a time to worry. I would talk to her about it another time. It was a moment to celebrate our final day in this warm and certainly welcoming country.

We ended our night at the Temple Bar with a toast led by Aiden:

"May the best of your past be the worst day of your future."

"What a beautiful thought. I love that toast. Slan-ta!" I toasted.

"It's *Slainte* Jules! God, I'm going to smack you." Filomena was laughing and came over to hug me. I love my SOFT sisters.

The men all serenaded us with 'Danny Boy.' The night couldn't have ended more pleasantly. I think we all felt the same, and I know that there would always be a wistfulness in our hearts when remembering our journey through Ireland.

A very late night at the bar didn't necessarily bode well for our flight to Italy the next day. We were all hungover. The three-hour trip was thus welcomed; even with flight nerves, the hours provided some much-needed rest in a fairly quiet environment. The thought of more alcohol was for once off-putting, and we spent the journey asleep instead of drinking. Even so, the man who sat behind me looked distinctly uncomfortable as we took our seats. A group of women, still smelling faintly of booze; I couldn't blame him, really. He pulled his cap low and slouched in his seat, ignoring the small smile I had shot his way while putting my bag into the overhead compartment.

By the time we landed, we were all feeling rather refreshed, stretching out our limbs and soaking in the wonderful rays of sunlight. Everything about Italy—the smells, the sights, the heat—it was all perfect to me. Regardless of my life in Canada, Italy never failed to feel like home.

Alessandro had offered to collect us from Naples and drive us over to Positano; however, we had declined in favor of taking the train. He would be taking a couple of weeks off in order to come visit Fran in Canada. We didn't want to use up one of his holiday days, and we were looking forward to the train journey.

Seeing all the sights and soaking in the countryside and feel of our surroundings was absolutely wonderful, and excitedly we pointed out things we saw from the train window. I noticed the man from the plane was in the same carriage as us, still with his cap pulled low, but I pushed him from my mind, shaking off the slightly uneasy feeling he gave me.

Even Sophia, after a single phone call to her other half, had stopped worrying about the children and was laughing as we played "I think I want that house." It had been started by Camilla when she was small, but we had all joined in over time, and now it was fun to pick out the houses we would like, even without a child to nudge us.

"I want that one!" Filomena announced, pointing at a large barn standing alone with acres of fruit trees and livestock. We all laughed, doubling over as she pouted. "And what's odd about that?"

"As if you would cope with being in the middle of nothing," Fran sniggered. "There are no neighbors, and you would be getting your hands dirty. Not in the fun way either!"

"As if you would!" Filomena retorted.

"I think I would," Fran replied thoughtfully. "Imagine being as … loud as you want with no neighbors to complain." She raised her eyebrows and smirked. This was what I had missed, this time of laughter and connection.

Aside from the gentle ribbing and innuendos, the train journey passed much faster than I would have liked. I was enjoying the experience. The train trip reminded me of traveling when we were younger and more spontaneous. We sipped on orange juice and prosecco and felt the buzz of excitement as Positano came into view. I couldn't wait to photograph this magical place. I knew it wouldn't disappoint. After we settled into our hotel, the ladies opted to take a quick nap. I wasn't tired and left to explore the beautiful town.

Positano is one of the finest, prettiest places on earth. I never tire of the authenticity and picturesque landscapes. I knew that upon returning home, the memories of this place would remain with me, filling me with a nostalgic ache. Once in the warm and comforting grasp of the village, city life seemed so far removed and impersonal. For now, however, I could simply enjoy the peaceful and stunning surroundings.

I felt wonderfully content, gazing upon the seaside village. The warm sun reflecting off the Mediterranean bathed the place in an otherworldly light. I reveled in the passion and creativity that went into building such a town. I was moved to write. And the writing, fortunately, at least somewhat preoccupied me. It took my mind off of the fact that I was in the same country as *him* and yet so far apart still.

My journals became full during my visits to Italy, the words flowing effortlessly from my pen as if they possessed a life of their own. The things I loved most about "my" Italy were the little treasures and surprises that I would find along the way; I became very much an inquisitive child hungering for more. It captured my attention like no other place on earth. The town, its color, and people gave me something meaningful to reflect upon, and amazingly I didn't think of Sebastian or Anthony as often as I otherwise might have.

Positano is watched over by the Church of Santa Maria, marking the town with its dominant dome. The green of it was gorgeous against the pale yellow of the outer building. To me, it was as if the building represented that synergy between simplicity and nature. The spirituality of the building, surrounded by clusters of colorful houses, demonstrated how wonderfully blessed the village was. The villagers were all pleasant and friendly, happy to chat idly about the wonder of the fantastic food, the exquisite views, or an excellent winery that they knew of. I relished interacting with them; finding out even more about this place I had secretly come to think of as a part of me. Somehow, though, that was difficult to put into words.

The breathtaking sights and the almost magical aura that surrounded this place left me feeling exhilarated. To travel there with my SOFT sisters, and experience *la vita bella* was an amazing feeling, and one that consumed me with magic. My energy was truly renewed through bella Italia. I wasn't even thinking of him … or so I told myself.

For some reason, I felt drawn to enter the Church of Santa Maria. The spirituality, the raw beauty of the place. The ability to think clearly and just be myself. I felt a need to confess, and not in the vague and emotional way that I confessed in my journals and my conversations with Fran. I needed a Catholic confession so that I could explain what had happened and beg forgiveness. I needed Him to hear the truth, the whole truth. I needed to speak to someone who wasn't invested, who would hear me as I was, and how I had been. I needed to speak to God, but I also needed the relief of talking to a stranger who would never betray my deepest secrets and thoughts. I needed a priest.

"Forgive me Father for I have sinned. It's been two years since my last confession. Oh Father, I do feel a need to confess. I've been down a dark path where I've lost my way, and I need guidance and clarity. I beg for forgiveness; I've broken my sacred marriage vows, fallen in love with another man, and not only have I betrayed my husband, I've also betrayed my faith."

"Continue my child."

I took a deep breath and let it all out.

"My mother lived a good, full life. She was always seeking wonderful experiences. She took the blessings she was given and nurtured them until they bloomed into something more. She was able to find the balance between respecting the path she'd been given and making that path as beautiful and enjoyable as possible. I wanted to do this, I feel my intentions were pure, however misguided they may be.

"My mother's death still haunts me. I know that she's with me, but I can't feel her embrace or cry on her shoulder. She was always my rock, my compass. I still speak to her, and I still feel her presence. But being without her, having to experience the death of the woman who created me, who was everything to me, and taught me my morals and my religion … has been difficult. I knew it would happen; I knew that she would leave this earth. It's our one certainty in life. I knew that she had to be taken away from her suffering, and yet I'm guilty of focusing on my own loss rather than her memory. I know she exists inside me, but Father, it isn't the same. I think this was the catalyst for everything else that has happened since."

"I feel you are torn, my child, and want to confess to God."

"I do Father. I'm not a bad person; I've just done a bad thing. I love my husband. He's still the man that I bound myself to before the eyes of God. I care for him, even in times of difficulty. But somewhere along the path we've grown apart. We don't communicate as we once did, and this is something that I'm guilty of. I've allowed my bitterness and insecurities to get the better of me and mistook this as a sign to move in a different direction. I should have recognized this realization instead as a sign to work harder and build back the relationship we once had. I am trying.

"Father I've had an affair. I felt lonely and hurt in my marriage. In seeking the relationship that we once had, I found a connection with someone else. My husband doesn't know, and I don't know whether I'll ever be able to tell him. It would break his heart. I need him like I need air to breathe, and yet this other man draws me to him like a flower to the sun. I'm afraid because I love them both. Please, please, lead me to redemption. I want my children to remember me in the way I remember my mother. I want to make sure that no one has to live in the shadow of their struggles. I want them to know that they are worthy of love.

"I've learned the value of reflection, and of having someone to speak to, to confess to. I've so much love for my friend, Francesca. Thank you for bringing her to me. She listens to me without judgment. I hope and pray that all my sisters find the same kind of peace that I seek in this moment. Please, Father, forgive me and give me guidance."

The priest responded with: "My dear child. You know what you must do. You must love your husband unconditionally. You must use your mouth to speak words of love and devotion, and your body to love only his. Remember your promises in your vows. From this moment on, you must promise to express your love for him and lift him up in the way that he's worthy of. And, in turn, he will show you the same love and devotion.

"My child, you have lost your way, but God will forgive you and never abandon you. He too will never judge you just as long as you believe in His love. My child, for your penance I ask you to do three Hail Marys and four Our Fathers."

"Thank you, Father."

At that moment, I felt cleansed. If only I had known what was to come.

POSITANO

Traveling – it leaves you speechless, then turns you into a storyteller.

Ibn Battuta

I love spending time with my sisters. We are as close as any group of women can be. It always amazes me how much fun we have together, how easy it is to be around each other. We love our conversations about love, life, fear, and desire. We even share in the same dreams—about our futures, those we love, the places we long to go, the adventures we intend to go on—and with my SOFT sisters sometimes I do feel as though I can turn my dreams into my reality. They give me hope, and in return I would like to do the same for them.

Our journeys together have brought me to such beautiful places. Places that I shall cherish always. Places that I have discovered more of myself. It's the combination of being in their unique presence and beholding all of the amazing sights that really has helped me to heal and to understand who I'm becoming.

Julia

★ ★ ★

We woke up fairly early on our final day in Positano, but we didn't want to sleep the day away. A trip to the beach was in order and, so far, we hadn't managed to spend much time just lying by the water. We had so many things we wanted to do. Whenever we went on a trip, we tried to absorb as much of the culture and local cuisine as we could, which was why on this day we all emerged bright and early, with packed bags for the beach. We planned to spend the whole day there and watch the sunset. We would definitely find restaurants that provided better food than we had thus far had in the villa.

The gorgeous beach was mostly free of the usual tourist-trap establishments; we all preferred to eat authentic food rather than versions that had been butchered into some form of American equivalent. We ambled over to the bus stop, a small local bus that only traveled to the beach and a couple of neighboring towns. The queue was already long, so we smiled politely, huddling slightly to the side of the other waiting passengers.

Unfortunately, others didn't have the same approach. It was surprising to me that the man who jumped ahead of the line was Italian and didn't even give us a second look as he slid ahead of us when the bus came into view. "Slid" wasn't really the word for it. More like barged, banging into my shoulder as he passed.

"Mi scusi!" I called to him, pointing my finger. "You need to get to the back of the line."

He looked at me coyly through thick-rimmed black glasses. With his slicked-back hair and thin frame, the obtrusive glasses only served to irritate me more.

"Scusi?" he asked.

"Yes. That's what I said. Per favore, si metta in fila."

He lifted his arms in the air, pretending not to hear me, his expression blank and confused, gesturing back and forth between us. I folded my arms. "This is crazy," I uttered.

Francesca heard my muttering and came to my aid. Hurricane Fran always came to the rescue whenever she thought the rest of us weren't being forthright enough.

"Enough!" she roared, marching directly up to the Italian, and waving her hand in front of his face. Her voice was loud and clear, her gestures understandable in any language. "Excusa me! Who do you think you are? In Canada we do not cut in line. Our Italian parents wouldn't cut in line. And you, young man … do not cut in line!"

She followed up with a threat along the lines of, if he didn't move his own skinny ass, she would do it for him. Without a word, the man walked to the back of the line with his head down, as the surrounding group started to cheer. The skinny Italian sat a couple of seats behind us, fiddling with his camera quietly. He got off just before our stop with a swagger to his step and a smirk to Francesca as he passed her.

"Shama onna youa!" he yelled once the doors had closed.

Francesca replied with the universal gesture of "fuck you."

"I'm sure that's the same guy that was on the plane with us. He was on the train as well …" I said.

"If he is, it's just a coincidence. Clearly, he has good taste in holiday destinations, but he's still an asshole," Fran scowled. "If we see him again, I'll tell him what's what."

Sophia giggled. "I think you did that already."

We pulled away from the curb once more, and I went back to staring out the window, exhausted and lost in my thoughts.

Somewhere in my mind, I registered the irritating man lifting his camera to focus on us as the bus left, but I couldn't quite bring myself to care. If he wanted to take pictures of women on his travels, that was fine by me.

There were still so many more places nearby that I wanted to visit and explore. Every time I went to Italy, a longing brewed in my heart for more. It wasn't just the surrounding culture, it was a calling to be back there, to exist in the place that I was born, and that my parents had called home. My soul felt drawn to the beautiful land, as if I still belonged there.

I felt drawn to Italy in the same way that I had been drawn to Sebastian. If he was my soul mate, Italy was our joyful palace. We ruled as our unapologetic selves. Italy was ours, and yet I needed to make it a place for Anthony and me to adore together. I hoped beyond all hope that bringing Anthony to a place that I connected to so wholly would allow me to connect to him in such a way as well. The romanticism of the place, our heritage, the sun, wine, and the good food—we were drawn to these things. We had always been drawn to many of the same things. And now we would find out whether that was enough to rekindle the passion I knew still had to exist … somewhere.

The coast of Italy is home to lemons, lots and lots of lemons, cultivated in an exclusive area of Amalfi known as the Garden of Lemons. As these are used to produce limoncello, it seemed only right that we drink the sweet liquor while we bathed on the beautiful beach. We had stuck mainly to wine throughout our Italy trip so far, and we quickly found ourselves feeling tipsy and youthful, requesting round after round from Genato, our personal butler for the day. This had been a shy request from Sophia—to enjoy a day on the beach while being waited on by an attractive shirtless Italian. Judging by her smile, Genato was everything that she had hoped for.

We had switched to prosecco by the time Francesca announced she was hungry; she ordered a pizza with hand gestures and a rather terrible Italian accent.

"Francesca!" Sophia exclaimed. "Why are you talking with an Italian accent?"

I subtly took a large sip from Francesca's glass. She could definitely do with pizza before she had more to drink.

Francesca winked. "Genato, can-a … we-a get-a … som-a … olives too-a?"

Genato just laughed and topped off our glasses, saying, "Si signorina, do you appreciate the olives?"

"Oh si, si. I appreciate … a the … a olives very much-a!"

Genato smirked and rattled off some sexually suggestive sentences at her before walking away to sort out our food. We were laughing, speculating over what he had said when Alexandra blurted out an observation that had all of us blushing and giggling.

"You know, I think we look better than ninety percent of the people here."

"Of course we do," commented Filomena. "We look damn good for our age."

Oh, we had definitely had a few drinks. It felt perfect, the most amazing girls' trip to date. Completely at ease, laughing at the slightest thing, enjoying the sights, the food, and the prosecco. We spent so much of our time being busy, working, raising families, and looking after our husbands that we didn't get as much time for ourselves as we really needed.

We nibbled at the delicious pizza and olives throughout the afternoon, requesting some bruschetta when the sharing boards started looking empty. Having a chance to just lie in the sun and write with good company made it my favorite day of the trip so far. I had enjoyed everywhere we had been and everything we had seen, but this was peaceful.

"So, what are you going to do when Anthony arrives?" Alex asked me. "I'm assuming you have got an itinerary planned."

I almost told her no, just to see her panic on my behalf.

"Yes," I assured her. "I've tried to include everything that makes Italy magical. I want him to love it here as much as I do."

"You haven't packed the days too much, have you? Sophia asked cheekily. "You need to leave aside time for … other things." She punctuated her obvious insinuation with a wink; I blushed. I had considered that, but I also didn't want us to have any long stretches of time that would become awkward. I felt that Anthony coming to Italy was a lot of pressure. I wanted him to see everything I had told him about, but I also wanted to make sure that he would enjoy the trip as well. I had thought long and hard about every activity, pulling together primarily a list of things that Anthony would enjoy. Many of our interests were the same of course, and it was my hope that we would enjoy them together.

I was anxious though. What if Anthony didn't have a good time? I wanted him to connect to Italy, as I had done. I had been so reluctant to have him join me, considering my history with Sebastian, and … well, I just really needed him to enjoy it. I needed *us* to enjoy it. I needed to remove the memories of Sebastian and make new ones with Anthony.

"I think I've got a good balance of activities planned, and some fabulous wineries along the way," I replied vaguely.

Later, we had dinner in one of the restaurants along the beach. How we were still hungry was beyond me; we had been eating and drinking all afternoon, and yet a simple spaghetti alla Nerano, a specialty dish from this area, called out to me from the menu. My sisters started talking about home and their lives in general. It was a special moment; I realized with a stab of guilt that I had been so wrapped up in my own troubles that I hadn't really asked about them.

"I hope the kids are okay," Sophia sighed. "I don't want them to feel like I've abandoned them."

"Why would they think that?" Alex asked softly, wrapping an arm around our youngest sibling. "You're a great mother, and it's good for them. They need to learn that you can have your own life, and a woman doesn't have to just stay at home and look after their family. If they see you taking time for yourself and enjoying your time in Italy, hopefully when they are older, they will do the same."

Sophia nodded and took a deep breath. "I know, that's what I keep telling myself. It's just that I feel as if I have to give them guidance all the time. We all know how important a parent's influence can be, and Bobby is so busy at work. God, I wish Mom was here. I'm still struggling with not having her around … I really wish they had their nonna's guidance too."

"They see you as a perfect mom Sophie. They love you," Alex told her firmly. "And that's also a good thing. Mom would be so proud."

"We all miss Mom," I added gently. "She was always there for us. And she loved her grandchildren. I know she's not here for your girls, but we can all tell them about her through stories, and we have a lot of those my sister!"

In truth, I had been spending precious, but too little time with my nieces. Recently, I had only seen them at events where we were all there, or if they were around when I went to one of my sisters' houses. I hadn't spent as much one-on-one time with them as I should have done. We had all known that Sophia was struggling, and I knew that I could have eased the burden a little. She was trying to advance in her career as a life coach after having her children, and she didn't really have the luxury of foregoing a career while they were young and then returning at a later date. She was working part-time helping Bobby, while trying to be there for them not only as herself, but also filling the space left by our own mother. Sophia reacted to the loss by trying to fill the void, wanting her children to have everything that we had and more. She was a great mother, but I really wanted to see her get some confidence back. She was way too hard on herself.

"I'll also have them whenever you like," Filomena chipped in. "I miss having the small ones around. It's not the same when they have all grown up." She had been suffering from empty nest syndrome for a while, and I pulled her into a tight squeeze.

"You will have grandchildren to spoil soon and to keep you on your toes," I reminded her.

She sighed, "Yes, I will. And I'm looking forward to it. It's just strange to think that my little girl is going to have a baby of her own. I miss having kids around all the time; it was our job, our life, you know?"

"Well, you can always help Fran with her mysterious business venture," Sophia ribbed. "Not that any of us are privy to what it actually bloody is."

"I'll tell you when the time is right," Francesca replied, laughing. "Besides, I've got other things going on …" She waggled her eyebrows.

Filomena lifted her glass in a salute. "I hear you, sister!"

They exchanged lewd stories all journey home, making the rest of us laugh and gasp with shock at some of the things they had apparently experienced.

RAVELLO

Se è tardi a trovarmi, insisti, se non ci sono in un posto, cerca in un altro, perché io son fermo da qualche parte ad aspettare te.

(If it's late to find me, insist, if I'm not in one place, look for another, because I'm standing somewhere waiting for you.)

Walt Whitman

Ravello is truly beautiful, more beautiful than any landscape I could conjure. A majestic town, known for its enchanting gardens, it's as if it comes straight from a fairy tale. I can see the mountains on a clear day, and the beautiful juxtaposition of the elegant town with the crashing waves fills me with a romantic yet tragic joy.

Ravello was once home to the likes of D. H. Lawrence and Gore Vidal, as well as a holiday home for Virginia Woolf. The birthplace of such classics as *Lady Chatterley's Lover*. Ravello is beautiful in history and meaning, not just visually. So popular among writers and artists …

One day I would love to have my own little villa here, to write my own stories. How wonderful would it be? To be remembered for my work here; to be "Julia Bello, who empowered women with her stories of strength and love."

Julia

★ ★ ★

I awoke the next day determined to enjoy Ravello while ignoring the voices inside my head aligned with my yearning for him—the mere mention of his name or memory of his face made it so very difficult for me to push those thoughts aside. The man shattered my world into a million pieces, whether he was with me or not. I could never return to the woman that I used to be. My world would spin around him. Regardless of all that had passed. Regardless even of whether the stunning Morgan was with him.

I was soon to see my husband and reconnect with him, and yet I knew that jealousy was seething down deep. That young blond thing ... she was everything that I wasn't, and therefore everything that I wished I could understand, and occasionally wished that I could be. Did Sebastian prefer her? He had after all left me to return to Italy, and over the years, apparently, he had always returned to her side. Obviously, she was important. I wasn't going to ever compete. That was a game I definitely was too old to play.

I had planned that day to see the lovely historical Villa Cimbrone, the crown jewel of Ravello, originating back to the eleventh century. The views are best from there, and it's rich in culture and mystery. But before that, my thoughts were interrupted by Francesca entering my room, two coffees in hand.

She kicked the door shut again behind her and came to sit on the end of my bed.

"Good morning," she sang, handing me a coffee. I sighed happily as I inhaled the lovely smell of waking up.

"Morning," I replied. "Thank you for bringing me coffee."

"I thought you might need it ... are you alright, baby girl?"

I gave her a wry smile. "Of course, why wouldn't I be?"

"Well, you know ..." Fran shifted and gave me a wink. "With *him* living in this country. I know you won't run into him, but I know you're probably worrying about it anyway."

I took a heavy-hearted sip of my drink.

"I can't help it," I admitted. "Honestly though, it's not as if we're magnets. We're not going to run into each other simply because we're in the same country. And, what start the whole vicious circle over again? Don't worry Fran, that is a mistake I have made many times. Lesson learned and I promise you, I won't go look for him either."

"I know, lovely," she patted my leg. "Remember, Anthony will be joining you soon, so you will only be alone for less than a week. Sebastian isn't going to be anywhere near you, I think you need this alone time, and you can just enjoy yourself exploring on your own, relaxing, writing, or just drink some vino until you pass out. Works for me when I want to forget sometimes."

I couldn't shake the feeling that she was wrong. I'd had a feeling of someone watching me pretty much the whole time we had been in Positano, and then I'd had a weird dream ... I likely wouldn't have been awake before Fran entered my room if it wasn't for the shock of it. A montage of places and activities, all focused on Sebastian, and seeing him in Ravello. Why did that bother me now? I had been in Italy for days without issue. I had essentially pushed all thoughts of him aside, I had even managed to admit to my faults, and struggles and, at least in spirit, swear him off, and break our emotional bond for good. I hoped it was simply a remnant of my decision and confusion, and it would fade away.

I had said my goodbyes to the girls last night when we returned to the villa, and I now hugged Fran a little extra tightly. I was so grateful for her in my life. The villa was quiet, and the town deserted as I got into the taxi and prepared for the next phase of my journey.

An hour later, I was settled into the small rustic stone villa that I would be sharing with my husband. Then just a couple of hours after settling in, I was leaving to explore again, camera in hand and sunhat on.

It was a long, steep walk up to la piazza but the fresh air in my lungs was exhilarating, and the thought of the famous villa spurred me on. It really was a sort of pilgrimage, a sacred journey to a place of sanctuary, a place where my literary heroes had shared a moment of calm after a tumultuous storm. This space offered them a wonderful landscape that soothed their souls and cleared their minds so that they could produce work that was beautiful, and authentically human.

Ravello was truly magnificent, and I felt hypnotized by its energy. I knew that when I returned home, I would miss the exquisite colors of the blues and turquoise of the Tyrrhenian Sea. The sunlight was hitting the cobblestones, paving the way for tourists, lovers, and writers like me. I was at one with Ravello; it would remain a part of me for the rest of my life.

Every look toward another person, every shared smile was a connection, and it filled my heart with joy even as I, and many others, walked the path alone. One million steps, all worth the altitude to arrive. Perched on top of a cliff, a poignant reminder of the importance and sanctity of a writers' retreat.

I continued to photograph the essence of Ravello as I made my way through the maze of cobblestone streets. I took my time, framing every shot carefully. Every photo that I took in this medieval town would tell a story, that of this magical place. I didn't want to simply take a picture of a building or a beautiful fountain, I wanted to capture the movement, the history. I wanted to show how it all blended together so perfectly.

I noticed a young woman lounging against a stone wall, enjoying a Toscanello cigar. I immediately started to photograph her until our eyes met briefly. I quickly tucked my camera away and bowed to her with a nod. She surprised me with her perfect English: "I love your shoes."

I smiled sheepishly. "Thank you so much. I hope you don't mind my taking photos. You just looked stunning. I wanted to capture your synergy with the surroundings. You remind me of a story."

"That's quite okay," she grinned and winked. "I'm flattered. Shame I'm not wearing makeup."

I laughed with her. She was young; her gentle blush reminded me of my daughters.

"You look wonderful as you are, darling. Don't let anyone tell you otherwise," I told her.

She ducked her head and stubbed out the last of her cigar.

"Thank you," she said shyly. "I hope you continue to find what you're looking for. Have a nice day."

"Thank you and, yes, I think I finally have."

Looking around again, long after the girl had left, I was still enraptured by my surroundings. Its grasp on me was powerful and comforting too. I felt a sense of home in this place, and

I knew, at least I hoped, it somehow would change my and Anthony's lives.

Italian architecture is just so beautiful. I wanted to capture it with my lens because I was captivated by everything I saw. Old doors, iron gates, enchanting gardens … everything made me wonder about the lives and stories of people who had inhabited these spaces. It seemed like fate, the gardens of hydrangeas, lavender, and geraniums. They reminded me of my mother. She had loved her garden and it loved her back; if I closed my eyes for a moment it was as if I could smell her perfume—she was beside me once more.

I was drawn to an old villa covered in vines that looked as if it belonged in another world. I stopped only when the back of my neck suddenly felt prickly; I thought I heard someone calling my name. Who here would even know me? I walked toward the sound but saw nothing. I must have imagined it; yet why did I feel disappointed? Had I expected Sebastian? He had infiltrated my thoughts often since we parted ways, but I pushed him from my mind in favor of quickly scanning through my photos as I continued through the gates.

I wandered the whole circle around the villa until I found a delightful secluded area of greenery behind it, complete with a view of the mountains and sea from the cliff's edge. I moved closer to the edge, as I let the beauty of the moment sink in, closing my eyes for a moment and savoring the brisk ocean winds against my face, and the feel of my hair fluttering around me.

I stepped forward, seeking the source of my enjoyment. Could anywhere be closer to perfection? The air grew warmer, and I felt drawn to the sounds of the sea and the wind that rushed through me. I took another step, only to hear a shriek behind me, quickly followed by a tornado of panic.

It was that sound that startled me; bringing me back to reality just as I felt my feet leave the ground. I was starting to fall. My camera dropped, and my eyes grew wide. Everything that had been so still and so peaceful only a split second before was pushed away in favor of the scream that rose in my throat and the thudding of my pulse.

"Julia!"

There was the sound of my name again, but this time the voice was familiar and comforting, and I longed to cling to it and hold it close, to bring that all-encompassing sound with me as I started to plunge into the water below.

"Julia!" The voice called again, and I frowned as I realized that I wasn't falling forward but backward. Strong arms wrapped around me and pulled me back with incredible force; I landed flat with a thud on the soft grass of the garden.

"Julia! Julia!"

I gasped, struggling to get a hold of myself. Fear controlled me, and I felt overwhelmed with the expectation that I was still going to die, that I still would feel my lungs fill with water after the impact of my body crashing against the rocks. Which would be worse? Would it matter when I was dead?

"My love!"

The voice called me back to the surface, and it seemed an angel was before me. A halo of golden sunlight framed his face, his hair falling forward, shading his pained grimace. He was pale, his eyes full of fear as I blinked to clear my vision to take in the mouth that I never thought I might see again.

"Sebastian …" I whispered. "Oh my god! What are you doing here?"

"Saving your life…again" he replied in a rather snarky tone, but relief was now evident on his face. Never in all the time we had spent together, had I seen him so wild with panic. "What were you thinking to put yourself in harm's way like that? Standing on the edge of a cliff. How could it be that I already lost you once, and now I was going to lose you again?"

He ran a hand roughly through his hair, suddenly seeing how close we were, how he was lying on top of me. He sat back on his heels but placed his hand on mine.

"Are you alright?" he asked.

"I'm fine," I managed to say, and pulled my hand back from his. I scrambled to lift myself into a sitting position, while I pulled out grass from my disheveled hair. "You didn't answer my question. What the hell are you even doing here?"

"Watching over you," he replied, his voice subdued.

Joy and anger rushed through me simultaneously. Could this man really still care for me after all that we had been through? But why did he think it was okay to follow me? I had felt someone following me for days; my paranoia had been correct. I should have listened to my gut.

"Sebastian," I repeated. "Why are you here?"

"I had to see you, Julia."

"And you thought stalking me was the way to do it? After deliberately leaving me, for her, and crushing me with your rejection, you thought following me, months later, would be a good way to go about it?"

"I never meant to hurt you, and I didn't leave you for her," he replied in a smaller voice. I longed to comfort him as he continued. "I couldn't put you through everything all over again, but you were here, in Italy. You were so close that I could touch you, and I just wanted to watch you for a while, to tell myself that I'd made the right decision, to leave you so you could live your life in peace. I just wanted to see you, my love, and know that you were okay."

I coughed gently and looked to the side to find a small group of people awkwardly watching our display.

"I think we should talk about this somewhere else," I suggested.

His eyes followed mine. "Yes, my love, I think so too."

★ ★ ★

There was a definite distance between us, as Sebastian and I walked to a nearby café close to the villa. I shot a quick message to Fran while the waiter sat us at a secluded table outside. I felt guilt bubbling. And yet I had nothing to feel guilty about. I was simply going to have an espresso with a friend I hadn't seen in several months, who just happened to save my life. Nothing to be guilty about. Nothing at all!

We sipped our coffees in near silence, only pausing when our waiter asked whether we would like some tiramisu. Our eyes met and I knew he was thinking the same thing as me. The memories of eating it together, licking the treat from the same spoon, sent jolts of desire through both of us. Soon though, the cold wave of reality took hold, and it was with a cordial tone that I offered to invite him back to the villa with me so that we could talk properly, and in private.

Never had I been more relieved to be away from home. How would it look for my husband to arrive, days after I spent time with another man, my former lover, nonetheless? Regardless of the distance between us, the connection was still there, and it would take a blind man not to notice the chemistry that Sebastian and I still had between us.

We had nothing to say; it was as if we were both afraid to start the conversation, suddenly too awkward to ask and answer really important questions. Instead, we resorted to small talk.

"How is Matteo?" he asked me, inquiring about the wedding and my daughter-in-law. I asked about his daughter. I told him of my plans to write a book, and how my sisters had all suggested that they be characters in my novel. He suggested that he could be too. Nothing like a hint of realism to make a book really connect. I sighed and thought of my journals, carefully documenting our relationship and my struggles with my relationship with Anthony. Couldn't they be formed into a book that would inspire and comfort? Was anyone else in the world going through what I was? I knew that I would have loved to have read something so honest and know that I wasn't alone.

I made the mistake of opening up a bottle of Brunello that I had purchased for Anthony. As we sipped our wine at the dinner table, not daring to sit beside each other on the sofa, we continued to talk for hours about life, books, and poetry, just like old times. And when it came time to call it a night, I told him he could crash on the sofa. He was certainly too drunk to drive. I got him settled with a blanket and pillow and showed him where the wood was in case the room got damp. The stone villa was beautiful to stay in, but even in the summer months it needed a fire to keep you from getting too cold.

"Goodnight Sebastian," I whispered.

"Goodnight," he replied, and quietly added, "Thank you. Sleep well, my love."

THE VILLA

The supreme happiness of life is the conviction that we are loved—loved for ourselves, or rather, loved in spite of ourselves.

Victor Hugo

Sometimes life doesn't give us any option as far as which direction to take. I believe in fate, that things will always turn out the way they are meant to be. I do seek guidance for my choices, and I try to abide by the laws of doing what's truly right for me. My meeting with Sebastian was fate, wasn't it? Or had it also been temptation? Had I been swayed from one path to another? If I had, then apparently that path was now the one I was destined to take.

Julia

★ ★ ★

I awoke the next morning before the sun rose, my toes cold and my arms wrapped tightly around my torso in a comforting hug. This damn villa had been so damp and may have been a mistake to rent. But it was so hauntingly beautiful, and that was what drew me to wanting to stay here. I didn't remember any of my dreams or any thoughts that had plagued me, but I had slept poorly, nevertheless, tossing and turning through the night. It had taken me long enough to drift off, knowing of Sebastian being downstairs, steps away from me, keeping me awake long after we had said goodnight. He was so, so close to me, that at times I swear I heard him breathing. All I needed to do was go back into the living room and touch him, and I knew that he would take me with open arms. Immediately upon waking, those thoughts came back, filling me with both guilt and anticipation. I couldn't act on those feelings, no matter how much I wanted to.

I was restless, and now I knew that I wasn't going to get back into my slumber, particularly not while being so cold. When I made my way to the living room I only shivered more. The stone walls that had been so homey and comforting during the day were haunting and looming at night. The villa was absolutely beautiful to look at, and yet so flawed when beheld in a different light. Much like people, I mused. People like me, Sebastian, and Anthony.

I heard him on the sofa, shifting behind me and I jumped, coming face to face with my once-lover. He was standing so close to me, smelling so familiar. I wanted to run my fingers through his messy hair and fold my body into his for warmth.

"Why do you look so cold?" he asked huskily, eyes still bleary from sleep.

"Because the fire burned out," I replied. I quickly turned away, determined to hide the blush that had spread over my cheeks. I stepped aside, to allow Sebastian to pass me. He reached for an iron poker and some logs, stoking the fire back to life. His silhouette was strong and masculine, framed by the damned stone walls, reminding me of the quintessential Byronic hero. Was Sebastian truly a Rochester or Darcy? I wasn't his savior; I couldn't be. While he had brought back the spark in me, I knew that I would never be able to do so for him. I couldn't be his Elizabeth or Jane. I wouldn't be the woman that was his loyal, adoring equal. I was bound by my marriage vows, by the family and history I shared with my husband. I belonged to someone else, and I always would.

This didn't stop the shiver of a different kind that shot through me as I watched the muscles of his bare back move as he worked, and the stray strands of hair that rested on his cheeks. He was wearing his jeans from earlier that day, and the sight of his ass hugged by the denim made my pulse race, a purr of pleasure forming in my throat. I could feel it in my loins and warmed up instantly with the thought of his touch. Suddenly, the fire didn't matter anymore. All I wanted was to run my fingers across his chest, lean against his back, and rest my palm on his beating heart. I was immediately intoxicated, the mere sight of him doing something so domestic filled me with all the feelings that I had hoped would pass.

I knew that once Sebastian came into my villa, I would be inviting him back into my life again, and yet I had held myself in denial. After all, the man had saved my life, again. He had saved me emotionally, and now he had also saved me physically too. I owed him more than any other person on earth, made all the sweeter by the knowledge that he would never see it that way. He would see it as his privilege, his duty—the simple act of caring for and protecting the woman that he loved.

He leaned toward me; I almost cried at the familiar scent of his cologne. I used to keep aside the dress I had worn for days after our dalliances, just so I could breathe in his intoxicating smell whenever I missed him. I had missed him a lot, and if Anthony had ever noticed my strange behavior around the laundry room, he never said a thing.

"My love," Sebastian's voice rumbled. "What are you thinking about? You're crying."

He slowly lifted a hand to my cheek and brushed away tears; I hadn't realized I had started to cry. I sniffed quietly and swallowed thickly.

"Just …" I struggled with my words, choking as tears threatened to take over. "How naive and reckless we once were. And yet after all our sweet promises, we weren't meant to be."

He sighed sadly and pulled me close, kissing the top of my head. I could feel his warmth, hear him smelling my hair; I shuddered against him.

"Why did you leave me?" I sobbed angrily. "How could you? You promised never to hurt me."

"Oh, my love," he whispered, clutching me tightly in his arms. He clung to me as if he would never let go, and I sunk into that comfort, desperately holding on as a woman struggling to keep her head above the tumultuous waves. I pushed him away and crossed my arms, shielding myself from his magnetic effect on me.

"You made your point clear, Sebastian, the day you decided to leave without discussion," I hissed. "You said you would never hurt me and yet you did just that. You didn't even stay to talk to me face to face, you just left!"

"Julia, my love, every smile, every touch, every act of love that you showed me, made me feel more than I ever thought I could. You made me feel the way you saw me; you made me into a man who could love again, and who could trust … again. I wanted you so badly. I just couldn't stay away from you. I was drawn to you, as a moth to a flame. You're the purest, most amazing thing to ever enter my life. Can you blame me for being selfish and wanting you all for myself? I needed you and you were with him! I finally realized, you will always choose him over me.

"You must understand, I never meant to hurt you. I would rather take a knife to my own heart than see you hurt. We grew together, my love; with every whispered word and gentle touch we drew closer. I didn't want you to end up hating me if your family broke because of me. I knew that I had to protect you at any cost. You had a life already before me. I had to stay away from you. I couldn't allow you to be tainted by my fucked up world or be hurt by my family. I didn't want you to become a part of the life that I've grown up in. What kind of man would I be if I brought you into such a world of lies?

"I thought if I were to disappear, you might move on. Maybe forget me. I thought you could remain as happy as when we were together, without my darkness otherwise consuming you. I'm sorry I broke your heart, but in doing so I also broke mine. As much as I try, I'll never be able to forget you, and I'll never forgive myself for hurting you. I won't ever be able to let go of you completely, but how much worse would my world be, knowing that you slowly came to resent me? How awful it would be to know that my choices could hurt you. And so, I condemned us to what I thought was the lesser of two evils.

"I'm sorrier than I'll ever be able to confess, but Julia, I would do it all over again. I would experience you as I have. Your taste will forever remain on my lips. You own my heart; do you understand me? Amore mio, ameró per sempre."

I sobbed louder, not caring about how ugly I might sound. This man loved me with the entirety of his body and soul. He wouldn't love me any less for the raw, human nature that I displayed as I bared myself before him. Anthony would be here in less than a week. My head was spinning. Why now? He wanted me to forgive him and take him back on the very trip that was supposed to bind me to my husband once again.

"Anthony is coming here. Damn it Sebastian! I can no longer bear the pain of loving you both. I'm so frustrated, confused, and exhausted! Why is this happening now? Our love was always like a tornado, crashing through me and bringing me high and low like the sea on the stormiest of nights. You continue to tear me apart, Sebastian, only to somehow put me back together more whole than before. Jesus, don't you understand? Don't you see what we're becoming? You and I changed as a result of our love. We believe in our love so much that we changed who we were to make it work. But this kind of love is destructive and will eventually tear us both apart, and one day we won't be able to fix ourselves again. Is it worth it to you?"

I slouched forward, no longer able to continue looking at him, this man that I was ripping into with my words. I needed to not fall into his arms again. I needed to stay strong.

"I won't be distracted by my feelings for you anymore. We both need to move on," I told him, but my voice faltered, and a lone whimper left my throat. I prayed the tears wouldn't take over. I needed him to believe me. I needed this to be the end. How could I refuse him once more if he offered me his undying love? My resolve was gone in a flash, my energy spent. He swept me back into his embrace, bending his knees to bring our faces level with each other. He stared at me, *into* me, and I was consumed by his fiery gaze.

"Julia, amore. I do understand you, but I'll always hope. I can't change your life, and not being together as one with you is something that I'm afraid of. I'll never be happy without you by my side. I can't make you stay. I can't make you feel things. I can't force something if you're not wanting it too. But I think I know why you're afraid to love me the way I love you. Because you're afraid of how strong you do love me, maybe even more than him. You and I are the same and you are as messed up as I am.

"My love, the only thing scarier than getting it wrong, is getting it so right you suddenly have something bigger to lose. I can't give up hope. To give up hope would be to stop living. Ti amo, Julia, and I'll do so until my last breath."

I clung to him, pressing tightly. All of my reason, all of my confidence was gone. My soul was ripped raw. For a few tense moments we simply stood, holding each other in front of the roaring flames, no sound but the crackling of the fire and our ragged breathing.

Sebastian moved tentatively, brushing my lips with his tenderly, slowly. He withdrew just as he had leaned in, and I let out a small mew of displeasure, even as I gave a halfhearted push against his chest. We shouldn't, and we both knew it.

"Sebastian …" I started, but he stopped my words with a simple press of his forehead against mine. How could I fight something I couldn't see? I felt so much for this man, and I was dizzy from my desire and the need to kiss him.

"This is so wrong Sebastian."

"It always was my love. Do you want me to leave?" he replied.

He lifted my chin to kiss me once more, only to pull back before I had a chance to reciprocate. I knew deep down that regardless of the romantic atmosphere, the hauntingly beautiful villa, the flicking light of the fireplace, we would have ended up here anyway. No matter how much time we spent apart, no matter how pure our intentions, we would never be able to be together without being one. We would always be able to find each other if we wished it so. We did love each other. And if it wasn't for my devotion to Anthony, I knew I would be able to stay with Sebastian forever.

"No," I reached for the back of his head, pulling his lips toward mine and flicking my tongue out to lick along the line of his surprised joy. His gaze was heated with desire, and I let out another small moan before the tornado came. It was immediate, the breaking of the dam. He pulled me close, lifting me as if I was weightless. He stepped toward the stone wall, stumbling slightly. I could feel it thrum through him as it did me, our bodies shaking in unison as we fought to move our clothes out of the way. When he slid inside me, he was firm and familiar; it was as if everything had led to this moment, and when we finally curled up on the sofa, our clothes scattered over the floor, I thought that if I could stay there, resting in his arms with my head against his chest, I would.

God knows I would.

GROCERY STORE

My bounty is as boundless as the sea,
My love as deep; the more I give to thee,
The more I have, for both are infinite.

William Shakespeare

How can I choose to prioritize one love, and then remove another entirely? The loves of my life have always felt different. I never felt as if I was replacing one love with another, and that's why it's so difficult to choose.

Why should my relationship with Anthony disallow a relationship with Sebastian? My love for Sebastian doesn't make my love for Anthony anything other than what it is—a deep, lifelong commitment bound by a piece of paper and religion.

No matter what happens between us, I will always love him and always want him to be a part of my life. We share children, family, memories. They are as precious to me as my own life. Beyond all emotion or physicality, Anthony is the man with whom I held my firstborn child. The man

I saw at the end of the aisle, surrounded by our family and friends. I gave Anthony my love, my everything. I also gave up my identity for him. If he could ever understand that my love for him is forever changing and still true, and that I didn't go looking for another to love …

But being loved by another man has given me a new life. Sebastian fills me with a joy that feeds a different part of my body, mind, and soul. In another world, I would remain with both of them forever, secure in my knowledge that I love them both with all my heart. But I know there can only be one, and I must make a choice, so that I can live the best life possible for me. For one, that means leaving him for good, as I will continue to love one man with my heart and the other with my soul. One will be my salvation. One will be my demise.

Julia

★ ★ ★

After making love again and hours of talking, Sebastian drove me to the grocery store late the next morning. We had decided to have dinner inside the villa away from prying eyes. We both welcomed the distance we needed to think through the events of the night before. He kept an arm wrapped around my shoulders, and I snuggled in tight, feeling as if somehow these were our last hours together.

My plans with Anthony weren't changing. Sebastian hugged each curve of the Amalfi mountainside gracefully, smoothly, lulling me as I sunk into my thoughts. Finally, and seemingly too soon, we arrived at the store.

"My love," Sebastian whispered, "I'll drop you here, you go in, and I'll park the car. I have a phone call I need to make."

"Okay. Will you be coming in too?" I asked.

"Yes amore. I won't be far behind."

I walked into the little grocery store on the mountainside. The charming yet dated place exuded a 1920s ambience—crates full of farm-fresh vegetables and fruits scattered all over the floor, creating something of an obstacle course.

The owners of the store politely welcomed me as I walked through the tattered and worn screen door.

"Salve signora, posso aiutarla?"

"Sì ho bisogno di un po'di frutta e verdure."

"Signora, I speak a bit of English, what is the fruit you desire?"

I loved how Italians could make even asking for fruit sound as if you were going to make love to it. Back home you would never hear the word "desire" in your local grocery store.

"You speak English, that's wonderful."

"Sì, un po; just to get me by signora."

"Well a little is all you need," I replied with a wide smile.

I discreetly watched the door, wondering whether Sebastian would join me soon. I wondered who he had to call? I knew I would feel disappointed if he didn't come in. I thought about Francesca, knowing that she would be worried about me. I had texted her to say I had met Sebastian but nothing more, and I hadn't been able to respond to any of her subsequent text messages. When I had turned on my phone that morning, I had seen several yet to be answered.

The owner had his young son gather up the fruit and vegetables on my list. I made my way over to the pasta selection and searched for the kind needed for my recipe that evening. My back turned to the door I didn't hear Sebastian come in. It was definitely surprising when I suddenly felt the intense heat behind me. He was up against me before I had even acknowledged his presence, slowly grabbing my waist from behind, pulling me back toward him.

He whispered nonchalantly in my ear, "Did you miss me, my love?"

He kissed my cheek as the gentle glide of his hand journeyed along the ruching of my dress. The moment became a soft silhouette of eroticism as his hardness pressed into me. Sebastian's right hand had now found a way into the slit of my skirt and his fingers brushed casually against me. My wetness made him moan.

"Don't make any sounds my love, or they will know that I'm touching the American woman," he teased.

I did as I was told. Pleasure shook my whole body. His fingers caused a rippling sensation that left me gasping for air. I quickly attempted to regain my composure upon hearing the faint accent of the proprietor in the background.

"Signora, did you find what you are in need of today?"

His son made his way over to pick up the pasta bags I had dropped to the floor as my lover was having his way with me unbeknownst to all. I turned slightly to see Sebastian's eyes connecting with mine. The reflection of his troubled soul blazed through his piercing green eyes and immediately dissipated just as I quickly remembered how dangerous and exhilarating he was.

All thoughts of worry vanished as I smiled at him. His handsome, rugged face and boyish grin made me want to drag him outside to the car and finish what he had started. His every touch, smile, and whisper were bringing me closer into his world and farther away from mine.

"My mind is overwhelmed with thoughts of what I want to do to you. Woman, you're the death of me, and I would welcome that death, knowing that I've consumed you completely," Sebastian purred, his hand now resting on my hip. Two women entered the store, and I felt myself shrink with uncertainty as I pushed back to lean into my lover's embrace. The women were muttering to each other, both of them looking strangely in my direction. There was no way that they could have seen what just occurred. Were they jealous of me having such an attractive companion, or did they perhaps know my lover?

"Sebastian," I replied softly, ignoring the grumbling pair. "When I'm with you, it's as if time stands still. I have no other thoughts but being with you—no reservations. I'm simply unable to act or behave normally."

My words were truthful, and I surprised even myself. The old me, the me before Sebastian, would have felt intimidated and humiliated by the events that had taken place and the clear adversaries that had entered the shop.

He took my hand, brought it to his lips and brushed it with a kiss.

"Amore, why would you want to behave any other way? Now, let's finish up in here so you can finish what you started when I get you back to the villa. What else to do you need?"

"Wait! What *I* started? You practically had me as a prisoner up against the pasta shelves. And I was distracted from my list, so we still need wine."

"You're the temptress, and a very good one. I'll take care of your packages and select some wine. I suggest you go outside and get some fresh air. You will need it."

I giggled and could feel my cheeks blush. I attempted to compose myself, as I knew the women in the store were still looking at me. I walked by them and couldn't resist.

"Signore, lui vale ogni centesimo, il suo nome è Sebastian."

They both turned red. I whistled at Sebastian and gave him the traditional Italian wave of "ciao ciao bello" as I walked out. I decided I would take the opportunity to call Francesca quickly.

"Julia! Honey, where have you been? Honestly, not answering my messages like that. What the fuck is going on? Oh my god! You slept with him, didn't you?"

"Fran, I'm fine, honestly. I'm sorry I didn't message you, but I got so lost in our conversation that I didn't realize the time. And, no I didn't sleep with him … yet."

Why was lying so easy for me now? It was as if I actually believed I was telling the truth. I used to dislike people like me. Now I had become one of them.

Fran was clearly not happy with me; I didn't want to disappoint her. Her voice had calmed down as she spoke.

"What the fuck Jules? I've been worried sick about you. Are you sure you're okay?"

"I'm alright, I promise. I'm sorry. We're just finishing up at the grocery store. Sebastian was kind enough to drive me here."

"I swear I'll kill him if he hurts you again Jules."

"That won't be necessary," I giggled, "and don't forget I did put him through hell, too. I'm not that innocent either. Besides, he's been nothing but a gentleman." There I went again, the word "liar" surging through my brain. "I'll call you tonight to talk more and fill you in on everything. I love you my friend, and I'm sorry I worried you."

"Love you more, Jules. This time don't make me wait; I don't care what time it is."

I loved all of my sisters and absolutely hated lying to them. Francesca, in particular, had never judged me, not even when I had told her everything about Sebastian and me. She was sad that I had reached such a point. She knew from her own experience that nothing good could come from living a lie, but she was also kind and understanding about what I was going through. I didn't know what I would have done without her to confide in, cry on, and eat gelato with.

I knew I would tell her the truth that night, but for the moment I would simply enjoy being with my lover. I turned and saw him walking toward me with my groceries. Even doing something as ordinary as carrying vegetables, he was so sexy. Eerily, I thought for a moment that he could pass for Anthony's younger brother. I quickly shook that thought out of my head. Sebastian's hair had grown longer since I had seen him last, and his beard was well manicured. I smiled as I remembered the rough feel of it as he kissed my skin. His white dress shirt and fitted jeans left little to the imagination and showed off his well-maintained physique. He looked calm and sleek, and very smooth on his feet. No wonder I hadn't heard him coming up behind me in the store—he was like a panther, patiently stalking his prey. You would never see him coming before it was too late, and you found your neck in the jaws of the beast. It was fitting that I felt so submissive in his presence, so willing to be his prize.

"What are you so intently thinking about, my love?" he asked.

"Sebastian, I was just coming back in to see what was taking you so long," I said to him, reaching out and resting my hand on his arm.

"Well Julia, I was negotiating a fee for my services with those women in the store. You're not only a temptress, but now also my pimp." He was smiling, and he winked and grabbed my hand to lead me to the car.

I couldn't stop laughing.

★ ★ ★

As he started the drive back to my place, I leaned my head back and shut my eyes. I was still trying to make sense of what was happening. We were lovers, forever doomed to be together in a whirlwind of emotion, or not together at all. For us, there was no in between, and it saddened me. No matter the other factors in our lives, our bodies and minds would be drawn together forever. Sebastian sensed my change in mood.

"Love, you're very quiet. Are you okay?" he asked.

In truth, I was overwhelmed by our afternoon rendezvous. Why was I so weak around him? How had I ended up in his arms again? I was stunned by all of it, and his seemingly innocent question sent me spiraling.

"Sebastian, damn you!" I yelled. How dare he? How could he not have the power to stop something that I could not? Didn't he know that I was powerless in his presence, unable to deny the sweet release that came with being together? I drew back my hand and lightly punched his shoulder. He hissed, swerving the car to find a proper place to park along the side of the cliff.

"Love, what's wrong?" His voice was soothing, but his eyes were full of fire.

"Oh my god, Sebastian. Why didn't you stay away from me." I hit him again and again, my fists pummeling softer and softer as I let the emotion run free. My tears started to flow uncontrollably, and he pulled me into his chest.

"Tell me with all honesty, will he ever be enough for you?"

"No!" I snapped, unable to stop the hurt I felt, given his words. Didn't he know that I hurt too? That it wasn't a matter of Anthony being enough, but my doing what was right? "I was just starting to accept the fact that you weren't coming back to me. And then you go and save my life … again! Tell me why you ruined me Sebastian?"

"You got it all wrong my love. You ruined me!"

"Why?"

"Because I love you, and you love him."

"No, you have it wrong Sebastian. I love you both and I can't do this to you or him anymore." I couldn't get it through to him. I wasn't finding the words, I suppose, to let him know the true depths of my feelings for him, how I yearned for him every single day, and yet I needed to consider my husband as well. They weren't separate, not for me. I did love both of them. And I needed both men, for very different reasons. How could I make him understand?

The rest of the drive back to the villa was silent, and it was with an air of finality that we said goodbye, neither of us speaking aloud the imminent decision.

★ ★ ★

I stood, overlooking the Tyrrhenian Sea, barefoot on the grass of the open garden terrace. I began to daydream about the allure of Sebastian's unspoken past, how dangerous his family was, and the threat of his mother. Did he have enough power to influence his mother to leave me and my family alone? Would he need to now that we had reached some form of closure?

I promised myself that trust would be of the heart, for there was no way he would have misled me with the promises he had made to always protect me. No matter what happened between us, Sebastian was a man of his word. I hoped beyond all hope that he recognized my tears for what they were—a sadness that a chapter of my life was closing.

I felt the gentle breeze from the sea caress my face and, for a second, I imagined Sebastian's fingers gliding slowly down the nape of my neck. The feeling began to fade away with the ping of my cell; I couldn't stop the weight on my heart when I saw that a few text messages from Anthony were coming through.

He told me of his excitement about traveling to see me soon. He was so excited, so willing to put this beautiful place into our memories, and yet, for me, Italy was now tainted. It was still so beautiful and meaningful, but in different ways. What was once a promise was now a bittersweet melancholy. I still had a couple of days to clear my head, but I didn't know whether that was enough time.

I was grateful that journaling my deepest thoughts and fears pertaining to my two loves had indeed helped me shed light on my own life and where I needed to be. It was a way of escaping the unknown. For the moment, it was all I had.

As I sat in silence back at the villa, the unspoken truths and web of complications began to unravel around me, knotting in new and tormenting ways. Was Sebastian's past so potentially dark and unsettling that I had somehow found other reasons to jeopardize my family? Why was this thought so unsettling? Would he run back to Morgan now? I had reacted so badly to Sebastian's on and off again relationship with Morgan. What right did I have to judge him? For months, he had been committed to only me, while I had split my time between him and Anthony. If someone else was bringing him solace, shouldn't I be happy, grateful that in my absence he wasn't alone? I had always known that we wouldn't have a happily ever after, or a traditional love story with us riding off into the sunset. No, what we had was a story of love and those never end well.

The villa still had his smell in the air. I paced up and down trying to push away the memories of Sebastian taking me against the wall, and the comfort of us cuddling like two lovers with thoughts only of each other on the sofa. The trip was supposed to be about totally reconnecting with Anthony, merging together the lives of the woman he had married and the woman that I had become. I had wanted him to understand me, and now I didn't know whether I truly understood myself. I wanted him to see the country that had transformed me, fostered my new self-awareness and confidence. I had struggled with both for many years, both in my marriage and outside of it. And now I didn't know that I truly had either.

I went outside for some fresh air and called Fran to give her an update. I told her the whole truth. I knew she would be relieved that I ended it for good with Sebastian. Still deep in thought, sitting on the ground among the clay pots of beautiful begonias, I heard footsteps crunching upon a few fallen twigs. I looked up, snapped from my reverie.

"Hi, Rafel," I greeted, smiling sadly at the villa's owner.

He smiled back, but his strange face provided me with no comfort.

"Buona giornata, Signora Bello. Pardon my intrusion, a courier just dropped this off for you at my office. He said it was of extreme urgency." I frowned. Was Sebastian trying to win me back? Could it be a message from Anthony?

"Thank you Rafel," I said, taking the letter from him. "You're never an interruption."

He waved, and I thanked him again as he hopped onto his bicycle. My hands shook as I opened the letter, unfolding the paper to reveal dark red feathered calligraphy. I felt sick for a reason that only took me a moment to connect. It was another threat. A letter from Daniela DeLuca:

```
I know you were with him here in Italy. If
you do not end it with him, the life you
once knew will change.

I reluctantly extend one more invitation to
desist in your pursuit of my son.

I will not be this generous again.

D. D L
```

For the first time since Anthony had laid his hands on me and pushed me, I felt a deep unknown fear. This wasn't a fear of my secret life being exposed, it was a fear for my life itself. Daniela had to be stopped. But how? I would have to tell Sebastian about his mother's threat … again.

REVELATIONS

Loving someone is giving them the power to break your heart, but trusting them not to.

Julianne Moore

One thing for sure is that being in this beautiful country I'm not myself. Since the ladies left, I have had time to think about who I am, albeit not a lot of time, but still, thinking in Italy is different.

My god, my life completely changed here … I didn't realize it then, but I fell in love … again … here! It's led me to believe that those most vulnerable to love are capable of loving more than one person in their lifetime. How can I not believe this to be true? I'm one of those vulnerable souls and I'm indeed capable of loving more than one man.

I have been in a committed and loving relationship with Anthony, and for the most part of our life together I have been happy. I had what everyone else wanted—I had monogamy and devotion—but as good and safe as my devoted marriage has been to me through the years, it's now left me feeling lonely, confused, and at times even downright crazy.

Lately, I have more questions than answers and I feel as if I'm surrounded by so many distractions and detours tempting me away from my so-called "normal life." I tried to stop a romantic relationship with Sebastian, but my reluctance only seemed to fuel our passionate love affair more. I couldn't get enough of him. I took risks and even put my family in danger, all for the love of a man I didn't fully belong to.

I read this quote somewhere by Junot Diaz: "The half-life of love is forever." How true are those words? I will love him forever. I still find it hard to grasp the truth sometimes, that I have totally succumbed to Sebastian for reasons beyond my comprehension, and still, deep down I knew I would eventually regret my choices.

Time is flying by. All I want to do is reflect back on why Anthony and I fell in love in the first place, and focus on how we can keep that love alive and, as God is my witness, I'm willing to do anything to survive through this confusing phase with my husband. I know something will reveal itself to me at some point.

After all, this Italian escapade with my husband was supposed to be all about us. Sebastian will always be my weakness. Being with him feels so right even when I know it's so wrong. He makes me feel things I have never felt before. What we had wasn't just about sex; we had a connection of the mind and soul, our bodies responded to each other's needs. People spend their whole life looking for that kind of love. Can it be that in some strange way I will always be devoted to him too?

Julia

★ ★ ★

I managed to pull myself together shortly before Anthony's arrival, distracting myself by doing all the things I had planned for us. He was engaged and happy, and I couldn't let myself crush that with my own emotional turmoil. He was particularly looking forward to the wine tour, and as it reminded me of our time in Montauk, I was excited too.

I brushed my hair and made sure my clothing and makeup were both classy and functional. While I wanted to look nice in a wine bar, I also didn't want to look ridiculous wandering through the vines. If we chose to have a nice walk afterward, then I also wanted to be prepared for that. Memories of my shoe destruction when in a similar situation with Sebastian rose up into my throat, and I forcefully pushed them aside. Today was for me and Anthony. Sebastian wasn't a part of it, and I was really looking forward to our last day and sipping Italian wine with my husband.

"Jules!" Anthony called, and I quickly pulled my boots on, zipping them up and smoothing down my shirt. I liked my look for the day and was so happy that I still fit into my jeans even if they were just a bit tight. I would get back to the gym when I got home. "The driver's here!"

"I'll be down shortly!" I called back, applying some sun protection balm onto my lips. The last thing I wanted was cracked, sore lips from our time out in the sun.

I heard Anthony opening the door. In the name of being polite I had to hurry, so as not to keep them waiting. I started down the stairs.

"Hey, how are you?" Although I couldn't see him, I could picture him offering his hand for the driver to shake.

"I'm good, how are you?"

My heart stopped. I froze on the stairs at the familiar voice. How could he be here? Again. Why? What would happen now? Had he come back to reveal us to my husband? Why would he, when he had sworn to me that he would always protect our secret life? We had ended it, but I had hoped that he had seen the inevitability the same way I did.

I rushed to meet them, tripping over the porch on my way out of the door. Both of my men rushed to grab me, and I felt faint, sensing them so close, each holding one of my arms.

"Are you okay?" Anthony asked me, a grin on his lips at the familiar clumsiness. Sebastian, however, looked concerned.

"I'm fine," I replied.

"Then why do you have a winter coat on?"

Both of them laughed at that, and I blushed as they stared at me. How mortifying. Here I was, on one of the warmest days of the year, and I had grabbed one of the jackets by the door that Rafael kept there for unprepared winter visitors. Shit. I tried to laugh it off, shrugging out of it and throwing it back inside.

"I guess I was in a hurry. I was trying not to be late for once." I pouted, and both men looked at my lips as if they would like to consume me. I gulped.

"How are you, Mrs. Julia? So nice to see you again," Sebastian stated so politely, and I shook slightly. I was saved from having to reply by my husband.

"You know my wife?"

"Yes," Sebastian replied. "I had her once, or twice."

I shot a glare at his deliberate innuendo. How dare he? I plastered on a smile and placed a hand on Anthony's arm.

"Sebastian was our driver when we celebrated Alexandra's birthday," I reminded him. "Two years ago, I think. Do you remember I told you about him?" I turned to Sebastian. "What a coincidence to see you again. I didn't know that you worked for this company, or in this part of Italy."

He shrugged. "Giovanni your original driver is a friend of mine. He is ill, and I owed him a favor. He asked me to help him out, so I took the job. I hope you're not disappointed."

His tone was teasing; I glared, but my husband replied first.

"Why would we be? Julia and the ladies have spoken well of you and your knowledge of the wine country, so I think we got lucky."

Anthony pulled me close, and I happily sunk into his side, praying that the day couldn't get any worse.

"Yes, lucky. Just my luck, lucky me! Ahh, I forgot my purse," I interjected quickly. "Let me just go and get it. I'm going inside to get my purse now."

"Is everything okay Julia? You're acting weird," Anthony said.

"I'm good Tony. I'll be right back. We need money to pay the man, don't we? It's in my purse and I'm going inside to get it, then we can go."

"Okay Jules, go get your purse then. Women … so confusing, eh bud?" He looked at Sebastian with a smirk and patted his back as they walked away from me and toward the car

I fled inside, immediately clutching up my purse and resting my body against the wall. I banged my head against it a couple of times, hoping that this was all a dream and that once I went back outside I would find my husband talking to another driver, some short grandfatherly man who would reminisce with us about when he met his wife and how much of a wonderful cook she was.

At least there would be wine. Thank god! And as our driver, Sebastian wouldn't partake. There was that. He never drank if he drove. I would get myself to the point of not caring, while not drunk enough to run my mouth off. We would be back before I knew it. How bad could this day be?

The drive to our first stop was utterly excruciating. Anthony and Sebastian chattered about trivial topics such as the weather and Sebastian's experiences as a driver. They were on to the topic of Canada, and how it compared to Italy by the time we arrived at the vineyard. I truly didn't know how I would survive more than one winery today.

"Here we are," Sebastian announced. "The first stop on our tour. Now, Giovanni told me that Mrs. Julia had a list of wine stops that she would like to include in the tour."

I turned to Anthony. "Go ahead love. I'll just give Sebastian the details for the other stops, and then catch up with you."

He leaned forward to kiss me tenderly on the cheek. "Try not to overwork the man, yeah?"

I shot him a smile. "I make no promises."

He chuckled as he walked off, and I whirled to glare at the man in the front seat.

"What the hell do you think you're doing?" I hissed. "This really takes the cake, Sebastian."

"Takes the cake? I've never heard that expression before. But, my love, I'm living in the moment," he replied. "That's what you told me to do."

"I can't believe you did this."

He shook his head. "You said that I was the best at my job. I didn't know that you spoke of me with your husband. What exactly did you tell him about me?"

"Nothing … it was Fran that raved about you, and Giovanni isn't sick!" I snapped. "God, Sebastian, you manipulated this whole thing."

"I needed to see you again," he murmured. "I needed to be close to you, even if I can't ever have you again. It's not over for me … yet. You can't always make the rules my love. This may be the last time I see you. Is that so very wrong?"

"Yes. Yes, it is."

"Cazzo, Julia. You're acting as if I committed a great crime here. I just wanted to drive you and show you more of Italy. No one can do it better than me."

"Oh, and you had no ulterior motive?"

He stared at me coolly and with a confident smile.

"I want to see you, to be close to you. I know that you're here with your husband. Nothing will stop me being close to you. You don't want me to leave; I can tell. You look at me with longing every time you see me. Your breathing quickens. Your cheeks flush. You still want me, Julia. And I'll be here for you until you don't."

"You think you know everything, don't you!" I spat. "Don't you dare even *hint* to my husband about our past. And my cheeks are not flushed! It's my blush. Damn you Sebastian!"

I slammed the door behind me, hurriedly making my way toward the building and my husband. I was there with Anthony, and I wasn't going to let Sebastian ruin our last day. I drank my tasters a little too quickly, and Anthony didn't seem to notice or comment. He enjoyed speaking to the experts about the different grapes used, and the best foods to pair with each of the delicious vintages. In contrast, I was quiet, lost in my thoughts. I smiled and gave my insight whenever it was required, and felt irritation run through me as I realized how my opinions of these fine Italian wines had been colored by the man waiting for us.

Even now, he had managed to get on my nerves. It took a full glass extra for me to begin to relax, and I suddenly felt myself smiling at my husband as he listened intently. He was so excited, buzzing with enthusiasm. For a moment, I was able to forget the terrible situation we were in. I wrapped my arm around his waist and smiled as he pulled me close. We bought a couple of bottles of his favorites we had tasted, then walked back to the car hand in hand, relaxed by the booze and the time spent together doing something that we loved. Wine was something that had drawn us closer over the years.

For a split second before Sebastian opened the doors, I thought I saw a flash of pain shoot through his eyes. I didn't want to hurt him. But what was I to do? He chose to be here. I was humming with wine, and it was easily noticed by him. He was driving us, and he knew that I would be with my husband. Besides, we were simply holding hands, not fucking.

With each stop on our tour, Anthony and I grew tipsier and laughed as we exchanged memories of previous wine tours. A niggling feeling settled in my gut each time we found ourselves back in the car, worrying that Sebastian would be distressed, or worse, say something about our love affair.

And yet I couldn't stop myself from leaning into Anthony's gentle touches or responding to his bright smiles. He seemed so happy. He kept his eyes on me the whole time, grinning as he lifted me over spots of mud and raced me through the vineyards. We frolicked as if we were twenty again. Maybe Italy truly could be a place for us to build new memories together and rediscover our love.

My worries faded as the day passed, and I began to melt into Anthony more and more, easily ignoring Sebastian as he drove us in silence. We snuggled in the back seat, and I pressed the occasional kiss to his arm. We decided that perhaps next year we would make the trip to Italy again, and bring the children with us.

By the time we arrived back at the villa I was tired, and my anxiety had risen to new heights once more. The wine buzz had tapered off, and I was left with a feeling of strong uncertainty, worried now about how I had been acting in front of my once-lover.

Anthony grabbed the bags of wine and entered the villa ahead of me, thanking Sebastian for his driving and suggestions before bidding him goodnight and saying that he would love for Sebastian to drive us again. I gulped and avoided Sebastian's gaze as he held my door open for me. He grabbed a hold of my hand.

"I love you still Julia," he whispered, and I looked at him, startled by the sorrow in his face.

"We've been through this," I told him. "I'm here with him. I'm sorry I hurt you. I never meant to."

He let go of my hand and swallowed. "I know."

We said our polite goodbyes and he barely looked at me. I felt that he finally understood that we were over. I watched him drive off, hoping that now we could both have closure. Once again, my heart was ripped open.

"Jules!" Anthony called. I took a moment to breathe as I put my bag by the door. I pulled my phone out and stared at it for a moment before turning it off. The last thing I wanted was to be distracted by any messages from Sebastian. I could grieve later; for now, my husband was calling for me.

I pasted on a smile and walked into the kitchen where my husband was preparing a light meal. I took the glass of wine he offered me. It was delicious, but not nearly enough to numb the pain. Anthony grinned at me as he sliced some bread and prosciutto we had picked up along the way.

"Wow, Jules, that was a fantastic day. Send me Sebastian's contact info. I'll recommend him to a client of mine who is coming to Italy next year. Thank you for planning such a wonderful trip. It was just like old times."

I reached for my glass again, and my smile became genuine. "We're good together Tony."

"Exactly. It's nice to finally get to spend time together, doing the things we've always loved. It really is." He placed the knife down and put some olives in a bowl before making his way over to me and pulling me into his arms. "I've missed you, Jules. I've missed having you to myself. I love you."

"I love you too," I whispered and drew him into a kiss. It was true. I loved him so much, and it made me so happy to have him feel the same way about our trip as I did. We were, finally, on the same page.

"Sebastian was an excellent tour guide," he added. "I really liked him. I can understand why you all spoke so kindly of him."

And just like that, my heart sank. Sebastian. Even now I couldn't escape him for long. My husband liked him. He would probably mention him when we spoke of our trip. Whenever we reminisced, there was a chance that Sebastian's name would come up. And if we came back? There was nothing stopping Anthony requesting Sebastian as our driver again.

I gritted my teeth throughout dinner, smiling and nodding, Anthony happily speaking for both of us. He even put forward a couple of ideas for other wineries we could visit and sites we could see when we came back. He adored Italy, that much was clear, but at that moment I felt drained and needed a break.

I placed my napkin on my plate and stood. "I'm exhausted. I think I'll take a bath," I told him. "I'll do the dishes later." I leaned over to give him a kiss; he lingered a moment longer than I had intended.

"I'll stay down here for a nightcap," he murmured. "Join me once you're done, or I can join you in the tub."

"You have seen this tub, and I barely fit in it, so the two of us never will. But, of course, I'll join you. I would love a Montenegro after."

I managed to relax amid the hot water and steam. By the time I pulled the plug, I felt the tension in my muscles and in my head had lessened, leaving me with a quiet joy. I slipped into my silk robe that Anthony loved so much and made my way downstairs to him. We'd had a wonderful day. I had just had a relaxing bath. It seemed a perfect time for us to end our last night together and connect.

"Tony," I called happily, skipping down the stairs to see my husband standing in front of the fire, glass of scotch in one hand and a letter in the other. His fist was tightly clenched and, just like that, so was my stomach.

What was so wrong? What news had he received? I already knew. It was the same type of envelope that I received earlier. Would Daniela really send a letter to my husband instead of me?

```
You have worn out my patience,

Stay away from my son.
```

Shit.
I waited for the storm to begin.

SECRETS

Hearts can break. Yes, hearts can break. Sometimes I think it would be better if we died when they did, but we don't.

Stephen King

My husband's face as he looked at me had so much pain. It was an expression that I had hoped I would never have to see. Shock. Betrayal. Hurt. Loss.

He now knew about Sebastian and me. He knew, and it had broken him, just as I had known it would. We had been through so much together, and yes, maybe he had hurt me over the years, but I had never thrust something so truly devastating on the man. I'd had a love affair for myself because I needed it to survive. It wasn't some sort of emotional retaliation. I didn't go looking for another man. Our relationship was something I needed. Passion, but not deliberate cruelty. I had tried to stay away from Sebastian. I had really tried.

Julia

I LOVE YOU STILL

★ ★ ★

Anthony turned to me properly, and I gasped with shock at the sight of photos. Photos of Sebastian and me in some very compromising positions. Photos, plural. Some of me and Sebastian here in Italy. How many photos? Who had taken them? My cheeks colored, not only at the delivery of the pictures to my husband, but also the thought that someone had been watching me all this time. My mind quickly went to the skinny man from the plane and the bus stop in Positano. Did Daniela have me followed throughout my vacation?

My world collapsed.

The photo on top had been taken in our home. The home that Anthony and I had built together. The home where we had raised our family. The world indeed stopped, and for a moment I thought that my heart had too.

"What the fuck is this?" he hissed; his voice was venomous. I flinched as he slammed his glass down onto the mantle; it smashed all over his hand. I longed to rush to him, to clean away the blood and promise that I would make everything better. But I froze on the spot, frightened by the hatred that emanated from Anthony.

"Anthony," I begged. "Please, listen to me …"

"What the *fuck* is this? In our home! In my fucking house!" He lurched toward me and I whimpered. "You fucked him in our bed. You slut!"

I shrunk into myself, praying that he would calm down, but not sure that I deserved his consideration.

"You fucking bitch! You were having an affair?"

I nodded, but he wasn't even looking at me. He was glaring at the photos, ripping them to shreds, and he threw them into the flames, watching them burn. He then turned back toward me and whispered, "You let me spend the day with him. With a man you fucked. Why are we even here? So you could get your little bit on the side?"

"Anthony …"

"How long has this been going on? How could you betray me like this? Do our vows mean nothing to you?" he roared back.

"Anthony, calm down," I begged. "You want to know how this happened? The last five years, you were never around. When I needed you, you weren't there. I ate dinner alone. I attended parties and birthdays without you. I had to tell our kids every time that you were too busy for a school play or to watch them play sports. I was *always* alone. You didn't want me, and I needed to feel truly wanted. I felt lonely and worthless in your absence. I found someone who helped me feel good about myself again. I didn't want to be the woman who drank wine at home alone, imagining all of the things you were doing without me. So many nights I waited for you to come home and acknowledge me, and you didn't."

"So, this is why you decided to sleep with him?" Anthony sneered. "How many fucking others were there?"

"None!" I cried. "Only you and him, only ever you and Sebastian. I know this is hard to understand but he helped me, Anthony. I was withering away. He made me feel alive again. I needed that so, so much. I needed to feel wanted; can't you understand that?"

"No, I don't understand! What the fuck. He made you feel alive?" he asked quietly. "In our home Jules? Wait … do you love him?"

I sniffed away my tears and turned away, trying to pull myself together.

"Jesus Christ!" he snapped. "Look at me Jules. Do you love him?"

My betrayal ran deep, and he knew it. I couldn't lie to him any longer.

"Yes, I do. I'm sorry Anthony, I do love him," I told him quietly.

He quickly lurched for me and raised his arm, and I closed my eyes waiting for the hit that never came. I opened them slowly to see him frozen in position, his own eyes dark, the darkest I had ever seen and brimming with tears. Slowly, he pulled his fist back down and started to sob. My strong husband. I had never seen him like this. He was always so stoic, and just like that, I had torn him apart too.

Anthony pulled me into his arms and held me so tightly, almost to the point where I had to struggle to breathe. He sobbed onto my shoulder, whimpering over and over again, begging me to tell him it wasn't true, that I didn't love Sebastian, that I had never loved anyone other than him.

I took his hands from around my waist and held them as he brought his forehead to rest on mine. His whole body was somehow limp and supported by mine; I squeezed his hands.

"Anthony, I'm sorry. I'm so, so sorry."

Both our warm tears streamed so heavily that they hit our hands, and he suddenly, abruptly, let go, turning away from me. He headed toward the door. Without looking up at me he questioned, "Tell me; how long has this been going on?"

"Just this year."

"How could you do this to me Jules … to our kids … our family?"

"Where are you going Anthony?" He didn't reply. He only slammed the door behind him.

Once more he was leaving the house drunk. I wouldn't chase him this time; it was different. Last time, he had left me. This time, I had driven him away. He wouldn't be driving; he would need to get a taxi. This time, at least he would be safer. But I didn't know that Sebastian would be. I rushed to my bag. My hands shook as I dialed his number, praying that he would pick up. Would he pick up if he was upset? I was sobbing fully by the time he answered, choking as I tried to speak.

"Sebastian. Oh, thank god!"

"Julia? Are you alright? What's happened? Amore, has he hurt you again?"

"No!" I cried. "It's Anthony … he hasn't hurt me. He knows about us."

The silence only lasted a moment, but it was deafening.

"Did you tell him about us?" he asked gently, and I cried harder at the hopefulness in his voice.

"No! Your fucking mother did! Sebastian … she had me followed and sent him pictures of us."

"I'm coming to see you," he said firmly. "I need to make sure you're okay."

"No! If he finds you here, he will kill you. He's so angry, and he's so drunk. He stormed out, and I don't know where he went. He might even be coming to look for you." I cried harder. "He will hurt you Sebastian if he finds you. Oh my god! What have I done?"

"I'll be fine, Julia. It's not your fault," Sebastian said softly. "It's mine. And I'll never be able to forgive myself, especially if he hurts you. Please stop crying my love. I'll take care of it."

I accepted his reassurance, but deep down I knew that it wasn't true. It wasn't his fault, it was mine. I was the married one; I had cheated on my husband, knowingly risking the life I had built with him for this love I never thought imaginable. I had put all of us in this position—and now, who the hell knew what was about to transpire? Sebastian said he would take care of it. I believed him, but that still didn't stop me from feeling terrified.

★ ★ ★

I was still shaking when I heard the sound of a car on the driveway. Which one of them was it? Would Anthony really hurt me? Or would Sebastian be there to protect me, risking his own well-being in the process?

I detected the sound of groaning, rushed to the door, and was amazed by the sight in front of me. Sebastian was pulling Anthony toward the house slowly, an arm slung over his shoulder, attempting to maneuver and shift the unconscious man. Both of them were covered in blood.

"Oh, my god …" I whispered. "What the hell happened?"

Sebastian grunted, and I moved out of the way so that he could deposit my unconscious husband onto the sofa. I rushed to my husband, torn between the two. Both of them were injured, but Anthony was unconscious, and I thought his nose looked broken.

"What happened?" I asked again.

Sebastian sighed and took a seat, frowning at the broken glass on the floor, and the smell of scotch that filled the air.

"He phoned me from a bar and asked me to drive him back here," Sebastian said.

"And you went?" I asked incredulously. "Honestly, what did you think would happen?"

"I thought he would get something off his chest, and I could apologize, and then I could hopefully drive him back here to make sure he was safe for you."

"Why are you both covered in blood? Why is my husband unconscious?"

Sebastian reached for my hand and I shuddered, though I allowed him to take it.

"Julia, I couldn't help it … I let him punch me twice, but I couldn't let him take the third swing. I just couldn't. I had to hit him back. I'm sorry. I'm so sorry amore. I felt his pain and understood his anger, and then when he hit me … it was like kicking a man that was already down. You see, Julia, he had you. He's always had you, and I knew that from seeing the two of you together today. I needed to recover some of my pride, and I couldn't just lie there and take it. I'm sorry, and I'll spend the rest of my life making it up to you, if you will let me."

"Sebastian …" I began, but he shook his head.

"It's alright," he told me and dropped my hand. "You need to tend to your husband."

"Don't go," I begged him. "Please. I'm just going to clean him up a bit and check on his injuries. Then let me tend to your eye; it looks awful."

"Of course, Julia. Whatever you like."

I filled a bowl with warm water and grabbed a clean cloth from the drawer, placing them next to my husband before rushing back to the kitchen to grab a bag of frozen peas. Anthony was still unaware of his surroundings, thanks to the combination of alcohol and a couple of right hooks. I focused on cleaning the blood away from his head. His face was swollen, and his lip was split. I placed the frozen bag onto his cheek and stroked his hair, praying that he would be alright.

And if he was alright, could he forgive me? Would Sebastian truly forgive me too, after all that had happened? I turned to speak to him, but Anthony began to stir.

He whimpered brokenly. I could barely understand what he was saying. "I loved you first, Jules." He tried to sit up and glared at Sebastian, trying to rise to his feet, but he fell back onto the sofa. "I loved her first. You son of a bitch!"

"I know you're angry," Sebastian replied. "But I loved her when she needed it most. I loved her when she was completely broken … by you. I loved her when she needed to feel treasured and alive. I gave her what you couldn't."

I felt as if the room had melted away, and the men were only talking to each other. I was watching, but for them it was as if I wasn't there.

"You're a bastard," Anthony replied. "What kind of man are you, to fuck another man's wife?"

I shrunk back. Anthony looked as if he might hit Sebastian once more, and I prepared myself to step between them.

"I didn't *fuck* her," Sebastian snapped. "I loved her. There's a fucking difference. And I loved her when you were ignoring her needs. What does that say about you?"

My heart ached as Anthony's eyes filled with tears. "I wasn't a good husband. I know that. But it wasn't all bad, was it Jules? We've had a wonderful life together, created a beautiful family. That's love. And even through all of it I always loved you. I need her in my life, our family needs her. I don't know how to live without her. I love her." With that, Anthony passed out again.

He was drunk, and I knew it, but his words still pierced me deeply. He loved me, even after he had found out about Sebastian. He had never stopped loving me. I was torn in two, pulled apart by each of these men.

Sebastian's eyes glistened as he rose to his feet; he approached me and softly kissed my forehead. "Goodbye Julia. I just wanted to bring him back to you," he whispered. "Should you need me, I'm only a phone call away."

The door shut quietly behind him as he left, and I took a seat beside my husband. Anthony muttered some more drunken words that I could barely understand.

"You can't have both of us. You need to choose, Jules. Me or him? If you come back home with me tomorrow, you will need to promise me. You can't ever see him again. Ever! Do you understand?"

I understood only too well. The time for a final decision had come. One lover would be estranged from me forever. One would remain with me forever. Whatever happened, after tonight I knew I would never be the same again.

THE CHOICE

Midway upon the journey of our life I found myself within a forest dark, for the straightforward pathway had been lost … I can't offer any good explanation for how I entered it. I was so sleepy at that point that I strayed from the right path.

Dante Alighieri

I struggled to sleep that night. Anthony was downstairs, and yet I had never felt further apart from him. My love for him, and his love for me wasn't enough to draw us together. We needed time for our wounds to heal and to repair the damage that we had caused each other. I longed to go back to how things used to be, but I knew I couldn't trade these experiences in. We had both changed, and I could only hope that we would survive our choices.

Julia

★ ★ ★

I tossed and turned, nightmares plaguing me. By the time I had finally fallen into a deep sleep, it was very late. I woke up to a pounding headache. I soon noticed that Anthony's clean clothes had been removed from the bedside.

Always more organized than I, Anthony would prepare his clothes the night before if he knew we were going to travel. Well, one of us had to be punctual. It was all just so normal. I felt as though no time had passed between us at all.

I rose from the sheets and padded my way downstairs, hoping Anthony had prepared coffee to drink before our departure. Maybe now we would start to make amends. If we could talk, just a little, before getting on the plane, I knew that would be the start of forgiveness.

Anthony wasn't in the kitchen.

He wasn't in the living room.

His suitcase wasn't by the front door.

He was gone. His words rang through my head: *You need to choose … If you come back home with me … You can't ever see him again. Ever!*

I knew then that Anthony had left without me on purpose. He had told me I had to choose either to join him on the plane or to stay in Italy with Sebastian. He had meant it when he asked me to choose, and he had given me space to do so. I sat down numbly on the floor, reaching for my phone.

```
Sebastian. I need you to come over. Please.

I'll be right there.
```

I let out a deep breath and hugged my knees; what I was going to say to him? How soon would he be here?

I wrenched the door open the moment I heard him arrive. He looked hopeful, but wary. His smile was the same beautiful, brilliant smile that I loved, and it hurt me that I had put him in such a situation, as it hurt me to do the same to Anthony. I took a deep breath and forced my body to calm down as we sat together on the very sofa that we had made love on.

"A piece of me will always belong to you, Sebastian," I began. "I don't know how I'll continue without you, but I have to stay with him. I promised to spend the rest of my life with him and I really don't think he would survive without me. I never meant to hurt him, or you. You, Sebastian, are and always will be a survivor. I never told you this, but I always thought that you didn't think you were worthy of love until you met me. I know I made you believe in love and I know you will also love again. You deserve to be with someone who can give you her whole heart. We were meant to cross paths, you and me, that I know for sure. We needed to give each other what the other needed to live and breathe again, but it was never meant to last forever. Please forgive me Sebastian and promise me that you will not close your heart to love."

Sebastian was so very quiet, and his smile had fallen throughout my speech, leaving him looking almost childlike in his unfettered sadness. He didn't try to hide his pain, only looked at me as if he were trying to memorize every detail of my face. He drank me in, and I yearned for him. But I couldn't. He knew now that I couldn't.

"I realized last night," he said softly. "You're needed in your current life, and I couldn't take you away from that. I just hoped, when you messaged me, that you ahh … my love, one thing I've learned is that no one gets through life without losing someone they love, someone they need, or something they thought was meant to be … at least in my life it's this way."

I reached out and pulled him into a hug, rubbing his neck to soothe him.

"Sebastian, you will continue without me, and you will find more happiness than you could ever imagine, I know it. You're the most loving, genuine, romantic man I've ever met. You made me feel alive, beautiful, and needed. Someone else deserves to feel like I have with you, someone who can give you everything, with none of the pain.

"Sebastian, sometimes you can love someone with everything you have, and it doesn't make any sense or mean that you belong together forever. It's unexpected, unknown, and unexplainable. But you take a chance anyway. You go for it, because most of the regret we have in life isn't for the words we say but rather the words that we don't say, always wondering what if. I'll never wonder what if with you. Promise me you will trust your heart again … it may surprise you. God knows mine did."

He nodded. "You will always be the one Julia. If I never love again, I can die a happy man because of loving you. I'll treasure your heart and, my love, you will always have all of mine. Now, please let me drive you to the airport. You need to be with him." His lips twitched into a lopsided smile.

"Are you sure?" I asked gently.

"Yes, my love. I want to do this for you. I took you away from your life, and now it's time for me to return you to it."

During the drive we held hands, like we had all those times before. This time it wasn't giddy excitement. It was saying goodbye.

When we arrived at the airport, Sebastian opened my car door, clearing his throat as he helped me out. He grabbed my luggage from the trunk and walked me inside to check it in. Even now, a gentleman.

He handed me our book, with that same lopsided smile that I loved so very much. I smiled too. *The Divine Comedy*, by Dante Alighieri. Inside the book was the inscription, written in Sebastian's familiar writing:

```
My Beatrice

Always Remember

Never Forget
```

"Never forget," he murmured as he pulled me close. "Never forget our time together. Always remember the happy times we shared, and our joy at finding each other. You have changed my life and I'll think of you often."

"I'll always love you Sebastian." I tried to smile but couldn't. My eyes filled with tears, and all I could do was caress his cheek with my hand as he took it and brought it to his lips; I felt his tears too.

"Amore, you brought me happiness," he said.

Our last kiss was a tender one; I wanted to never let go of him. He pulled away from me first and then turned before I could reply. I watched him leave. He didn't look back at me, and my stomach flipped as I saw him walk away for good.

I composed myself and made my way to the gate, immediately boarding the plane. It wasn't full yet, and I easily spotted my husband, head down and lost in his thoughts. He didn't see me walking toward him, and I stood in the aisle waiting for him to look up. I was afraid maybe he would still be angry and had changed his mind.

"Is this seat free?" I asked.

He jumped to his feet. Tears of joy slid down my cheeks as he immediately pulled me close, crushing me to his chest.

"Only for you, Jules. Always for you."

I sat down beside him. I knew Anthony and I had a lot of work ahead of us to repair what was broken. As we took off for home, I clutched my book from Sebastian in one hand, and my husband's familiar fingers in the other, praying that I was where I belonged.

THE DUEL

I never thought love was worth fighting for but then I look into your eyes, I'm ready for war …

Anonymous

Sebastian DeLuca

I didn't know what I was thinking when I went to the bar. *He* was sure to be pissed off with me, and quite rightly too. I had ripped his world apart in a way that I knew all too well. I had suffered awfully when I had returned to Italy, leaving Julia behind. It had been weeks of hiding inside, curtains drawn, scotch in hand. I remember that one day I had looked in the mirror, the unsightly growth of hair on my face, the pallor of my skin, and the redness of my eyes. I wanted to be strong and in control of my emotions, but I couldn't not grieve. To carry on as usual would do an injustice to the memories of our time together.

I also couldn't hide from what I had done. I immediately spotted "the husband" at the bar, knocking back scotch as if it were water. He had clearly been crying, and I shivered in empathy. To lose Julia, to feel like she was no longer yours …

I cleared my throat and stood up straighter, preparing myself for the altercation. He may knock me down, but I would stand tall. I would never apologize for loving a woman like Julia. Even if she was his wife. She was the sun in the sky, the moon in the night. She was the cool breeze on a warm day, and the last leaves on a tree in autumn. She was all that was beautiful and joyful in my world. Without her, the world turned to black.

The man was slumped over; it took every ounce of courage that I had to approach him and face what I had done.

Say it. I had never said it before, but now it was time.

"Anthony," I croaked out, acknowledging that he was real and whole, truly existing as a part of Julia's life. "Anthony, I'm so, so sorry for you to find out in such a way. My mother was way out of line, and I can't apologize enough for what she's done."

"What …" He shook his head and hissed. "What you have done! You bastard, you did this! It was *you*! And her! You can't blame anyone else for your actions. What kind of man are you? You took my wife, with no shame. You spent the day with me, in our company. What did you do? Touch my wife whenever I was out of sight? Did you take pleasure in humiliating me?"

"No. Never."

"Then why? Why the fuck did you do it? And why am I finding out now, from a letter, with explicit photographs of you fucking her in my home! I deserve better than that. I've cared for her, provided for her, and given her a family. What have you done? She's been my everything since the day we married. And now? I'm nothing to her because of you!"

He spat out, spraying my face with his anger. "You, you haven't been through any of that with her. You haven't been there when she was giving birth, or when her mother died. You have come along as a bed warmer, a fuck, and yet you traveled to Canada to do so? You're sick!"

"No! I love her and I won't apologize for loving Julia. Never. We may not have the relationship that you have, but our experiences are not any lesser. Our love is different, but just as strong. Your relationship is held together by familiarity and affection; ours is passion and connection. While yours is constant, ours is explosive. She's my world, much as she's yours. It's not possible to look upon her, to see her eyes, and not to love her."

"How dare you!" he snapped. "You fucking prick. Your relationship is *nothing* compared to mine. Your so called 'passion' will run cold, and then what will you be left with? A series of regrets and years wasted on a woman who was never yours. She will drown in guilt for what she's done. For your actions, she will suffer!"

"That's why I left her." I told him. "I left her to save her. I didn't care about you, or right and wrong; I cared about her and her love for you. I wanted her to be happy, even if she wasn't happy with me. Could you say the same?"

He paused before his eyes glinted gold. "That's not a concern of mine," he hissed. "I haven't had to think like that since the moment that we said I do. Unlike some, we believe in our vows. For you to get in between that, you're truly the devil." He stumbled to his feet and lurched toward me. "You're evil. She was happy."

"She wasn't happy," I replied coldly, tensing my body in preparation for an assault. "You weren't there for her. You may say you love her, but did you truly love her? I never laid a hand on her in anger like you did. When she was struggling, she came to me. When she was lonely, I had her. When she wanted emotion, connection, passion, she came to me. You weren't there when she needed you. You're not blameless in this."

"You fuck!" Anthony snarled and lifted his fist.

Don't move. You deserve this. Think how Julia has been hurt by this. Think how hurt you would be if you were her husband. You deserve this.

The crack of his fist against my face was like a burn that gave me a sick sense of satisfaction. Blood dripped from my lips, and I reveled in the feeling of absolution.

Help me atone for my sins.

He lifted his hand again, and it took all that I had not to flinch. The second impact hurt more than the first; I heard the sick crunch of my nose before the stream of blood.

Two hits. Two releases of my blood. Enough.

"You fuck!" Anthony yelled. "This is all your fault. You! You seduced her!"

He lifted his fist again, but I was too quick for him. I slammed my retaliatory strike into him, hitting his nose and left eye in one fierce blow.

It's not my fault. It is my fault, but he's not without blame.

Anthony fell to the floor, his head smacking the corner of a table. I felt nothing as I saw the cut, but then he began to sob in earnest, curling into a fetal position on the floor.

"I love her. I love her so, so much. I loved her first. I'm not perfect, but she's my wife. And you … you took that from me. You took advantage of her weakness …"

He whimpered and tried to get to his feet, but apparently the pain of his wound and the alcohol flooding through his veins rendered him unconscious. I wiped the blood from my face and stared apologetically at the bar tender.

"Per favore mandami il conto, pagherò per tutto," I told him. "I'm Sebastian DeLuca. I'll pay for the damage and his bill."

He nodded, not asking for my contact information. The name was enough. I hauled my nemesis away from the astounded masses and into my car, strapping him into the passenger seat beside me. The drive was going to be one of the longest of my life, even though the distance was short. I turned to my inebriated companion.

"You may have loved her first. I know that, now. I never realized how much you love her. Meeting you finally made you real. I only saw you in terms of Julia, a man who would hurt her enough to push her into the arms of another. She always told me that she loved you, but I never thought that you could make her happy.

"She means the world to me, just as she does to you. She's enchanted us, shown us a wonder and beauty that's unrivalled in this world, and I pray that you can forgive her for this relationship, this connection with me. I love her, and I want her, but I never want to hurt you. Now, I see you as a reflection of myself. We're the same, you and me. I know you would never agree with me about this. You see me as the enemy, but I see us as brothers. We've walked the same roads, run the same paths. We've both chased the love of a wonderful woman, without considering the consequences of our behaviors.

"You don't know this, but the real reason I left her to return here was because I didn't want her to be consumed by guilt. I saw her pain every time she left you to come to me. I thought that if she were to focus on you entirely, you would make her happy. I wanted her to feel whole in the life that was important to her. She belongs to you; she belongs in Canada with her friends and her family. To think she would remain with me is merely a dream. I felt so sure when she phoned me this evening. And then, to see how broken she was by you and your leaving, and how worried she was for you … I now see her love for you with my own eyes.

"A large part of me wants her to stay here. I want my world to be with her eternally bathed in sunlight, but I understand now that she may have only been a break in the clouds. I selfishly hope that she sees me as her salvation.

"Anthony, no matter what happens from this day forward … I love her still. And always will."

THE END

Back to Me

SNEAKPEEK

PROLOGUE

My name is Francesca Danese. I've been told that I am a good person, among other adjectives…strong, bold, courageous, exhibiting an unquenchable lust for life. All true I must say. Well, the "good" part, that is most definitely true. And do you want to know why? Largely, because I have lived my life with that echoing mantra, that voice prodding me to always please others, make others happy even at my own expense. Such was the case with my parents. I married the man they chose for me, the one they thought suited me perfectly. Love or lack of love, well, that didn't matter. Why should you love the man you're supposed to be spending the rest of your life with, right? So, I did as I was told, dutifully kept my mouth shut. And needless to say, things only spiraled downward from there.

This, consequently, became the start of my addiction to, for argument's sake, let's call them fixer-upper relationships. A rocky relationship often spun into a rockier marriage, and it was one bad marriage after the next. We will get to that though in my story… for right now, let's return to why I am a "good" person. My second ex-husband absolutely crushed me. Cheating on me with a much younger woman wasn't enough to crush me, or even the nights and nights of crying my eyes out. It was the belief that I could somehow make him see me as the better woman and convince him to stay with me because of it. How stupid was I to lower myself to such a level of self-value? And yet, if he were dying, I would still be there to take care of him, right by his side. Yes, even though he absolutely pulverized my heart, to the point where I needed a village to fix me—or in my case, my sisters. You could say they picked me up as only they could, cleaned me up and loved me back to life.

And then there is the other word people generally use to describe me: "courageous." To stand up against daunting odds and to do so without fear, that is my understanding of the word at any rate. Show me a person who says that they are never afraid, and I will show you a liar. We are human; it is instinctual when confronting the dangerous, the overwhelming or the downright terrifying. I never wanted to have to be courageous. However, with some of the paths I've taken, the roads selected in my life, I have had no choice but to be brave—to show that inner courage that I somehow managed to muster just when it was needed. I do believe that everyone lives the life they create for themselves. So why has mine seemed so toxic? And yet, the "toxic" just became my normal sadly. Until eventually I broke the spell, I severed the chain of toxicity and came to realize that once and for all I could be free—it was all right there, right within: that path BACK TO ME.

AND THEN WE WERE FIVE

*"Sisters make the bad times good
and the good times unforgettable."*

"I can't believe she's gone. Why would she do that? Why would she leave without saying a word to any of us?" I still found myself shaking my head in disbelief.

"Yeah, but just look at her in this photo—she looks fucking amazing, not to mention happy. Apparently, all it takes to uproot your entire life and leave everything behind is a smoking hot Australian yoga instructor and a little flexibility."

"Oh my God! Fran, that's so wrong to think that way. Her and Frank seemed so happy. They had such an incredible life together, well at least that is what we all saw. Right? She doted on him constantly. I am so confused," Julia said. I responded by pointing to a photo of Christy…

"Look at this picture! Doesn't seem to be the case. I am sorry to say this, but she looks fabulous and happy"

"Yes, she looks fabulous. Blah blah blah. I'm sorry I'm just upset that she neglected to tell any of us. I thought we meant more to her than that." Alexandra was right. She broke the sisterhood code; she'd let us all down. Christy had made her bed and would consequently have to lie in it (both literally and figuratively speaking).

"I just never thought one of us would do that, you know? It's just wrong. I agree with Alex," Philomena echoed.

To which I responded: "Well I am kind of pissed off to be honest."

"I have an idea," Sophia piped in, as the silent one of the group she had yet to offer her take on all of this. "Why don't we have a sage party. Start fresh—wipe out all the negative energy that she left behind."

Julia began to laugh, "What? Isn't that for homes only?"

I had to agree with Sophia here. We all could use a good cleansing of the sisterhood.

"Yes," I said. "You are right, but it's not just because she hurt us—I think we can all use some good energy in our lives. I know I certainly can. Especially after Alessandro. Let's do it! I'm in. I will get us ten sage sticks. We will have a party"

"Ten! I think one would do the trick Fran" Alexandra laughed.

"No make it ten; ten is good!" Julia added laughing as well. In fact, by this point, we were all pretty much laughing—a very good thing given the circumstances…TO BE CONTINUED

LETTER FROM MY FATHER

My name is Vincenzo Vecchio. I was married to the late Teresa Cubello on June 23, 1963. We had four children in our marriage. Our first, Lisa Maria, was born in Aosta in 1964. Our second, Modesta, was born in a small village in southern Italy in 1966. Leonora and Umberto were born in Canada in 1969 and 1974. I immigrated to Canada on July 7, 1966. After two months my wife came with our two beautiful girls, Lisa, who was two years old, and Modesta, who was only six months old.

Together, my wife and I did everything we could to raise our girls and our son healthy and bright. We are not a rich family, but we have good principles, with high morals and family traditions, honesty and respect towards others in the true sense of the word.

Modesta was, and still is, the daughter every family wants. She has never caused us any disappointment, and we are pleased with the rest of our children. Modesta was always the liveliest. She always had a sense of humour, even during the difficult times in her life. As a young adult, once she completed high school, she studied for two years in Toronto. After receiving her hairstylist diploma, Modesta, with my help, opened a hair studio, which she operated until she met her husband, Marino Tonan. They married and started a family based on the same ideals and values credited to us as parents. She gave us the joy of becoming grandparents to three beautiful jewels, Lucas, Isabella, and Ava. Modesta kept her family in great spirits.

Her mother, my wife, who passed away in 2012 due to a grave illness, was very fulfilled with her four children and all of her grandchildren. Especially with Modesta, who, due to her health issues would often keep my wife worried. I should write a novel about Modesta. My wife would be so happy to see Modesta write this book. Teresa lived for her and all of us.

I am now old, and many things I will keep in my heart. I just want to say thank you to my wife and all my children. To Modesta, I thank you for all that you have done and will do in the future. Keep your respect towards others and your moral values and teach them to your children.

Modesta, you and your family are always in my heart. I love you to death.

I am your father, Vincenzo.

CPSIA information can be obtained
at www.ICGtesting.com
Printed in the USA
LVHW102026260822
726876LV00003B/391